RESERVATIONS OF THE HEART

A SWEETGUM MEADOWS ROMANCE BOOK 10

IMANI PRICE

First Edition: September 2025

ISBN 979-8-89283-306-6 (ebook)
ISBN 978-1-962071-57-4 (paperback)

Published by Books to Hook Publishing, LLC.
www.BooksToHook.com

CONTENTS

CHAPTER ONE

The scent of warm gingerbread and spiced cider curled through the air, wrapping the cozy diner in a blanket of holiday nostalgia. Rochelle adjusted the collar of her deep-red sweater and took a sip of her eggnog, savoring the velvety richness. It had been months since she'd run this place, but stepping inside always felt like slipping into a well-loved memory.

A soft hum of conversation threaded the diner, blending with the sweet notes of holiday music drifting from the vintage jukebox at the far corner. The festive jingle of silver bells decorated the door each time a new guest entered, letting in a swirl of frosty air. Red, gold, and green garlands twinkled along the walls, while strands of lights created a gentle glow above the tables. Rochelle felt a surge of pride when she noticed how many patrons—young and old—were drawn here tonight for the warmth and camaraderie. Although she was technically retired, the life of the diner still felt like an extension of herself.

From behind the counter, Stan—the head baker—emerged with a plate piled high with fresh gingerbread cookies, their crisp edges kissed by the oven's heat. He set them down with a flourish, the scent immediately drawing a crowd.

"Well, well, well," Rochelle teased, setting her mug down. "I was wondering when the real holiday treats would make an appearance." Her comment earned a few laughs from the patrons gathered around, eager to grab a taste. "Now, don't get greedy. Let's remember our manners—older folks first."

"I like the way you think," Mei, her best friend of over thirty years, declared, sliding an arm around Rochelle's shoulders. Known to most as Mrs. Zhang, Mei was a force of nature, a woman whose presence could command a room as effortlessly as her silver bell earrings jingled when she moved. "In fact, Rochelle and I should taste-test these first. Just to be sure they're up to standard." She made a protective circle around the plate with her arms, flashing a mischievous grin at the younger crowd gathered in their Christmas sweaters.

"Stan, you have outdone yourself this year," Rochelle added, leaning in to catch another inhale of the cookies. "You must have sprinkled a little extra holiday magic in that dough."

Malachi, Rochelle's nephew and the new owner of the diner, leaned against the counter with an easy smile, his broad frame cozy in a snowman-adorned sweater. His fiancée, Aimee, had brought out homemade peppermint bark earlier, and between that and the cookies, the holiday spirit was in full swing. He slipped an arm around Aimee's waist, his love for her clear in the way he instinctively pulled her closer.

"You ladies are absolutely right," he said, lifting his hands in surrender. "Take as much as you like. There's plenty of holiday cheer to go around."

Rochelle met Mei's gaze, and with a knowing smile, they each grabbed a cookie. "To tradition," Rochelle said, tapping hers lightly against Mei's before taking a bite.

The familiar taste of molasses and cinnamon melted on her tongue, and for a moment, Rochelle let herself enjoy it—let herself be part of this warmth, this joy. The months had flown by, and with them had gone the rush of running this diner, the steady hum of purpose that had filled her days. Retirement had been an adjustment, and though she didn't regret stepping back, she hadn't quite figured out how to fill the space it left behind.

She glanced around at the little details only a former owner would notice: the crack in the tile near the old jukebox, the place under the counter where she'd once tucked extra napkins for busy days, even the old chalkboard where she used to write daily specials—still bearing her neat, looping handwriting in ghostly traces. Small memories pricked at her heart, sweet and poignant.

As the party buzzed around her, Rochelle leaned an elbow on the counter, watching the room unfold in soft, golden light. Malachi and Aimee swayed to a holiday tune playing in the background, laughter spilling from a nearby table where Alex and Maia, another couple she and Mei had helped nudge together, were deep in conversation.

"And that's what I love about small-town gatherings," Rochelle mused, taking another slow bite of her cookie. "You get to see people happy, right where they belong."

Mei hummed in agreement. "Although, let's be honest—we had a hand in making a lot of these matches happen." She lifted her eggnog in a toast. "We might as well start charging for our services."

Rochelle laughed, the sound warm and full. "You know, you're right. We're practically professional matchmakers at this point." She glanced toward the door just as a new group of guests arrived, their coats dusted with the lightest touch of snow. Among them, a familiar figure stood just a little taller, his presence somehow both steady and quietly striking.

Benjamin Walters.

Rochelle's breath caught momentarily, heart giving a single flutter. Benjamin was a kind of tall, dark, and sweet that quietly turned heads in a space that already felt merry and bright. He moved in that measured, thoughtful way she found both soothing and intriguing. The subtle flecks of silver in his close-cropped hair reflected the overhead lights, and she noted the gentle lines at the corners of his eyes—proof he'd done his fair share of smiling through life.

Her laughter stilled for a brief second before she quickly took another sip of eggnog.

"Well, look who finally decided to show up," Mei whispered, elbowing Rochelle playfully. "And here you were, convinced he wouldn't make it."

Rochelle rolled her eyes, though her stomach fluttered. "That man's got more important things to do than—"

"Than spend the holidays in the company of a woman who makes the best coffee he's ever had?" Mei finished for her, grinning. "Mm-hmm. Sure, Rochelle."

Benjamin made his way toward the snack table, exchanging greetings with Malachi and a few of the others. His dark blue sweater was simple but sharp, the kind of thing that made a man look effortlessly put together. The air of quiet confidence he carried hadn't changed, nor had the way he made people feel at ease just by being near.

He paused to admire the decorations Aimee had strung up: shimmering ribbons and holly berries winking in the soft light. His gaze drifted around the diner, as if taking in every detail, until it finally landed on Rochelle. Caught under his warm, appraising look, an unexpected bloom of sensation unfurled inside her, soft as the fairy lights overhead.

Mei wasn't even trying to be subtle now. "You should go say hi."

Rochelle waved a dismissive hand. "If he wants to talk, he knows where to find me."

And yet, she found herself watching as he laughed at something Malachi said, his smile slow but genuine. She had spent years making matches for others, guiding them toward happiness. Maybe, just maybe, it was time to consider what was waiting for her. She quickly stifled that thought before it could take firm root. She'd long ago decided that love was not for her. She'd never again put herself through the heartache she'd once experienced.

A wave of excited chatter rolled through the diner as someone turned the music up a notch—an old-school R&B holiday number that had folks nodding along. Rochelle absently tapped her foot. The aroma of gingerbread, pine, and the smoky-sweet of hot cider mingled in the air.

As Benjamin glanced her way, his eyes warm and knowing, Rochelle did something she hadn't in a long time—she let herself wonder *what if*.

CHAPTER TWO

Benjamin adjusted his cuffs, the thought of his gift under the tree grounding him as he navigated the festive chaos of the diner. Though the swirl of chatter, holiday tunes, and mouthwatering scents put him on edge—he was never one for large gatherings—something about this night tugged at him to stay. The air itself seemed alive, shimmering with the promise of warmth. Laughter and the scent of warm cinnamon swirled in the air, blending with the rich aroma of spiced cider. He had never been one for crowds, but tonight, something about the holiday warmth made him linger. Or maybe it was someone.

"Staying at Sweetgum Meadows Bed-and-Breakfast was definitely one of the best bed-and-breakfast experiences I've had," a young man in a turtleneck and coat said, showering Benjamin with praise at the snack table. "Your establishment has some top-notch service, Mr. Benjamin."

Benjamin offered a polite smile, nodding as he absorbed the compliment. The young man's enthusiasm reminded Benjamin of the early days of his own career, back when he'd worried every day about winning over guests with a sincere smile and soft-spoken charm. "I'm very happy to hear that you and your spouse enjoyed your stay." Benjamin accepted the compliment with a nod, though his focus was only half there. He had helped himself to a cupcake, but taking a bite was the furthest thing from his mind. The invitation to tonight's gathering had been personal—one he couldn't bring himself to turn down. Not when he knew Rochelle would be here.

"We did, sir. You're an impressive businessman," another guest added, rolling the sleeves of his sweater to his elbows. "Hats off!" With a final handshake, the two men drifted away, leaving Benjamin alone at the table.

Distant laughter, the clinking of mugs, the smooth hum of holiday tunes—it all blurred around him. Benjamin let his gaze travel across the diner's interior, admiring the garlands draped along the walls and the vintage lights casting a soft glow on every face. He noticed the older regulars exchanging stories in a booth by the window, and the younger couples sneaking shy smiles over steamy mugs of cocoa. The entire space throbbed with that unique holiday energy he'd almost forgotten he could enjoy. Rochelle had a way of standing out even in the middle of a bustling room. Even when she wasn't looking his way, she had a presence he could feel. And tonight, she seemed to glow, wrapped in an auburn sweater that made her skin look like the warmest, richest cocoa.

Benjamin's pulse quickened at the sight of her. He found himself recalling the first time he'd ventured into her diner—her easy laugh, the warmth in her voice, the immediate sense of home she brought to every corner of the room. He'd spent countless hours trying to convince himself he was there just for the coffee or the daily special. But deep down, he'd known better.

"Hey, I didn't know you made cupcakes! Why didn't you tell me, Aimee?"

That voice.

Benjamin turned just in time to see Rochelle hop off her stool and glide toward the table. His chest tightened at the simple act of watching her walk—there was grace in her every step, bearing witness to the self-assuredness she'd earned over a lifetime. He barely had a moment to steel himself before she reached for a treat, taking a bite with a delighted hum.

She licked a bit of frosting from her upper lip, eyes flicking up to meet his. "Mm."

Benjamin swallowed, suddenly feeling the heat of the diner more acutely. At once, the memory of that small, wrapped box under the tree came surging back to mind. His free hand twitched, as though itching to give it to her right then and there. "Hey, you." His voice came out smoother than he expected. "Didn't see you when I walked in."

She waved a hand, brushing it off. "I'm hard to miss." Her teasing smile made his chest tighten. "How you doing this Christmas Eve?"

"Doing well." A knot formed in his throat. He wondered if she noticed the momentary tremble in his voice. Later, she'd get her gift, the one he'd chosen with more care than he'd ever admit. But right now, standing here, watching her savor a cupcake like it was the best thing she'd tasted all season, he realized he was caught in something bigger than a simple exchange.

"I like your sweater, Ms. Rochelle."

"What? This old thing?" She tugged at the sleeve, the fabric soft and worn. "Just something I found in the back of my closet. Didn't want to steal all the attention at Malachi and Aimee's party. My time's come and gone."

Benjamin frowned, not liking the way she said it, as if the best of her days had already passed. "Your time's gone?" He picked up a small cinnamon bun to busy his hands.

She winked. "Oh, don't worry. This is only for tonight. Sometimes you gotta learn to step back for the youngsters to shine."

Benjamin chuckled, letting the sound roll through him. "That doesn't sound like you."

Rochelle's eyes flickered with something—something he couldn't quite name—before she tilted her head toward the farthest booth. "Shall we sit down?"

Benjamin followed her lead, grateful for the moment of reprieve from the energy buzzing around them. He trailed behind her, inhaling the lingering traces of ginger and spice that clung to the air. The lights felt a touch dimmer away from the bustling crowd, giving the booth a cozy, almost intimate atmosphere. Once they settled in, Rochelle wasted no time diving into a tale about Malachi's progress at the diner, how the party had come together, and—most intriguingly—how she was convinced Malachi was going to propose to Aimee tonight.

"They've been dancing around it all year," she said, shaking her head. "But I know it's happening tonight."

Benjamin sipped his hot chocolate, studying her. "It's always nice when a man finds his true love." His gaze flickered toward the Christmas tree, where Malachi and Aimee stood in the center of a small group. The way they leaned into each other, the way Malachi's hand stayed protectively on Aimee's back—it was love, clear and steady. "They say such a thing only happens once."

Rochelle's smile softened, her fingers tracing the rim of her mug. "And it's special when they find them this early." She let out a wistful sigh. "But enough about them. What about you, Benjamin? How have you been?"

Benjamin set his mug down. He could feel the heat of her gaze, both comforting and unsettling. "I could listen to you all day, Ms. Rochelle. Your stories about your business and adventures are always quite the treat." He meant every word. "Makes an old lonely man feel more included in something. Even if it's just by being a listener."

Rochelle's fingers curled around the warm ceramic of her

cup. Something unreadable passed over her face, something knowing.

He felt a sudden swell of vulnerability, recalling the quiet nights at his B&B when he'd stare into the empty fireplace, wishing he had someone to share the day's small triumphs and struggles. It was never quite the same after his wife passed, and though time had eased the sharp ache of grief, he wasn't sure if he'd ever moved on. Yet here was Rochelle, stirring feelings he thought he'd tucked away for good.

And then, the chime of a fork against a glass cut through the air.

Malachi stood by the tree, grinning. "Alright, everyone, it's time for the gift exchange!"

Excitement rippled through the room. People clapped, couples exchanged playful glances, and Rochelle's eyes lit up with anticipation.

"Finally," she whispered, elbowing Benjamin lightly. "Time to see who got what."

The faintest brush of her elbow against his side sent a gentle jolt through him, as if her warmth could cut through the snowy chill outside. As the first few gifts were passed around, laughter and exclamations of joy filled the room. Aimee beamed as she unwrapped a set of beautifully carved recipe cards. India from book club clutched a puzzle book to her chest with an over-joyed squeal. One by one, names were called, until only two presents remained under the tree.

Across the diner, behind the crowd, Benjamin spotted a young man named Jonah, a part-time worker at the diner who was grinning at him. Jonah offered a subtle thumbs-up—confirmation that their little plan had worked. Weeks earlier, Benjamin had quietly slipped Jonah a favor: if there was a Secret Santa list in the works for the holiday party, Benjamin wanted Rochelle's name, and he wanted Rochelle to unknowingly draw his. Jonah, eager to help and bound by no obligations other than a mischievous streak, made it happen. All these weeks, Benjamin had carried the thrill of that secret, uncertain if it would really come together. But here they were.

Malachi picked up the shimmering gold gift bag first, glancing between the guests. "Looks like this one's for..." His eyes sparkled. "Aunt Rochelle."

A murmur of amusement spread through the crowd as Rochelle made her way up, but Benjamin wasn't paying attention to them. His focus was on her, on the way she hesitated for just a moment before accepting the bag.

"And this last one," Malachi continued, picking up the second gift, "is for Benjamin."

A hush fell over the crowd, then a ripple of chuckles. Rochelle's brow lifted as she turned, holding her gold gift bag in both hands.

"Well, well, well," she murmured, a teasing lilt to her voice. "Looks like we got each other."

Benjamin's grip tightened around the present. He should have guessed. Maybe deep down, he had—after all, he'd planned for this. But nothing could prepare him for the tension in his chest, knowing he was about to hand her something that felt very personal.

Rochelle reached for his hand, squeezing it briefly before stepping back. "Shall we?"

They unwrapped their gifts together, laughter and applause surrounding them. Rochelle peeled back the tissue paper, slowly revealing a small, midnight-blue box. When she opened the lid, her breath caught. Nestled inside lay a delicate silver bracelet with a single coffee-cup charm—an elegant nod to her history with the diner. Engraved on the underside of the tiny cup were the words: ***Your warmth never left***. Her eyes glistened when she caught sight of the inscription.

Meanwhile, Benjamin carefully slid the ribbon off his present, his own anticipation thrumming through him. Inside, he found a beautifully crafted fountain pen with a subtle swirl of black and silver along its handle. Tucked beneath the pen was a small card bearing a handwritten note: *For the man who's written more chapters in his life than he realizes—may you keep writing new ones.*

Benjamin's breath hitched. A wave of emotion rushed through him as he read the note, picturing Rochelle painstakingly selecting something that symbolized both reflection and the promise of fresh pages ahead.

For Benjamin, the only thing he truly registered was the way Rochelle's eyes softened when she saw what he had chosen for her. The way her lips parted just slightly in surprise before curving into the kind of smile that made him feel like, just maybe, he'd done something right.

Benjamin's heart pounded as he watched the light dance in her eyes. He felt an almost boyish sense of triumph—relief that his secret arrangement with Jonah had worked, mixed with a slow bloom of hope.

And for the first time in years, Benjamin felt the possibility of something more.

CHAPTER THREE

he warmth of the holiday gathering lingered in the air long after the gift exchange had ended. After sharing the booth with Benjamin in the midst of the party, Rochelle found herself alone for a moment—he'd stepped away to talk with Malachi. The scents of cinnamon and nutmeg still clung to the air, mingling with soft Christmas tunes. Rochelle ran her fingers over the ribbon, her mind turning over what had happened.

She couldn't stop replaying it: the hush in the diner when Malachi announced she and Benjamin had drawn each other's names, the collective wave of delighted curiosity from onlookers, and the weightless flutter in her stomach as she peeled back delicate tissue paper. Even now, her fingertips remembered how gently she'd lifted the silver bracelet from its snug box. She could almost still feel the tiny coffee-cup charm glinting under the diner's golden lights—a tangible nod to a life she'd nurtured here.

Benjamin had picked out something thoughtful. Something that made her chest tighten in ways she wasn't sure she was ready to name.

Across the diner, he stood in quiet conversation with Malachi, his presence as steady as always. She had known Benjamin for years, but tonight, there was something different about the way he looked at her. Something deliberate. Something that made her feel seen in a way she hadn't in a long time.

"Now, that was something special." Mei slid into the seat beside her, a knowing smile tugging at the corner of her lips. "If I didn't know any better, I'd say that man put more thought into your gift than anyone else's."

Rochelle gave her a look. "Don't start."

Mei held up her hands in surrender. "I'm just saying, it's not every day a man picks out something so perfect for you. And it's not every day you look this flustered about it."

Rochelle scoffed, turning her attention back to the delicate bracelet nestled inside the velvet box. It wasn't flashy. It wasn't extravagant. But it was her. A simple silver chain with a small charm shaped like a coffee cup—a nod to the years she'd spent running this diner, to the thing that had always given her comfort.

Her gaze lingered on the charm, remembering the heady aroma of freshly brewed coffee that used to greet her every morning when she owned this place. The thoughtful detail made her chest flutter. Surely no one else would've known how much that meant to her. And yet...there it was, shining in her hands, as if made precisely for her.

She ran her fingers over the charm, something unspoken settling in her chest.

A stray thought crept in: was it truly chance they had drawn each other? It felt almost too perfect... Rochelle tried to dismiss the idea, telling herself coincidences happen. Still, the question lingered. Part of her marveled at the odds, while another part couldn't shake how deliberately he'd chosen that particular item. Maybe, just maybe, it was no accident, and she wasn't sure what to feel. She turned the charm over, her pulse thrumming with possibility.

"You going to sit here all night staring at that, or are you going to go talk to him?" Mei nudged her gently.

Rochelle sighed. "I talk to him all the time."

"Not like this."

Before she could protest, a familiar voice cut through the chatter of the diner.

"Ms. Rochelle."

Her breath caught for half a second before she looked up. Benjamin stood at the edge of her booth, one hand in his pocket, the other resting on the back of the seat. His deep blue sweater brought out the rich brown of his skin, and for a moment, Rochelle was struck by how effortlessly handsome he was.

She cleared her throat. "Benjamin."

His lips curved slightly. "Mind if I sit?"

Mei wasted no time sliding out of the booth. "Oh, I was just about to go check on something in the kitchen. You two enjoy." She winked at Rochelle before disappearing, leaving them alone.

Benjamin chuckled as he took Mei's spot. "She's not subtle."

"She never has been." Rochelle set the box down beside her and folded her hands on the table. "Thank you, by the way. For the gift. It was thoughtful."

His gaze softened. "I wanted to get you something that meant something."

The sincerity in his tone sent a soft warmth spiraling through her. She pictured his strong hands carefully picking out that little charm, the silver chain, maybe running through the details of her life in his mind. Had he genuinely foreseen she'd be the one to open it? She didn't know for sure, but it was enough to leave her heart fluttering.

It was such a simple statement, yet it pressed into something deep inside her. She searched his face, wondering how long he had been paying this much attention. How long he had been waiting for a moment like this.

"You really didn't have to," she murmured.

"I wanted to."

Silence settled between them, but it wasn't uncomfortable. It was full.

For years, Rochelle had watched love bloom around her. She had played matchmaker, nudged people together, and smiled as young couples found their way to happiness. She had always been content being a spectator, always convinced that her time had come and gone. But sitting here now, looking into Benjamin's steady, unwavering gaze, she wondered if maybe, just maybe, there was still something left for her, too.

She ran her thumb over the bracelet's clasp. Her heart pounded an unsteady rhythm as a new question formed: What if all these gentle gestures are meant for me alone? But she swallowed that notion, afraid to feed it too much hope.

Benjamin exhaled softly and glanced down at the bracelet. "May I?"

She hesitated, then held out her wrist. He took it gently, his fingers warm as he fastened the clasp. His touch lingered just a second longer than necessary, and when he looked up, something unspoken passed between them.

Rochelle felt the weight of it settle deep in her chest.

The chain felt simultaneously fragile and strong, just like the possibility that shimmered between them in this fleeting moment. She tried to keep her thoughts steady, but she couldn't stop envisioning him standing before a store display, picking out exactly what would make her heart soar. A flutter of nerves and excitement whipped through her.

The song playing over the speakers changed, something slow and familiar. Around them, couples swayed together near the Christmas tree, laughter and warmth filling the space.

Benjamin tilted his head toward the dance floor. "You feel like taking a chance on an old tradition?"

Rochelle arched a brow. "You dance?"

A slow, warm smile spread across his face. "With the right partner."

She let out a breath that was almost a laugh. Then, before she could talk herself out of it, she slipped her hand into his. "Alright, Mr. Benjamin. Let's see what you got."

As he led her toward the dance floor, the world around them seemed to soften. Maybe it was the lights. Maybe it was the music. Or maybe it was just him.

Whatever it was, Rochelle wasn't ready to let it go just yet.

CHAPTER FOUR

Last week's Icicle Festival had to have been the most successful one yet. Benjamin couldn't remember another time when every business in town had been brimming with customers. He recalled the swirl of bright lights against the snowy sky, the warmth of carolers' voices floating on frosty air, and the excited buzz of families skipping from one shop to the next, bags of trinkets and souvenirs in hand. Even the street vendors had made a fortune on tourists, their carts lined up along Main Street, scents of roasted almonds and sweet kettle corn wafting through the air.

Benjamin maneuvered his old-school vehicle through town, finally settling on a parking spot near Town Hall. The street was still packed, likely with business owners and locals lingering after the festival. No chance of finding a spot any closer to the diner.

He unbuckled his seatbelt, stepped out, and inhaled the crisp winter air. The cold didn't bother him much; he was layered in thick, quality clothing, a habit he'd formed years ago. His B&B's steady success meant he never had to think twice about restocking his wardrobe. Still, he'd kept a tradition—every winter, when new clothes came in, he made sure the old ones found their way to someone who needed them more.

He paused before locking the car, letting his gaze sweep the lively street. Despite the recent snowfall, Sweetgum felt more alive than ever—like it thrived under the pressure of winter chill. Laughter echoed from the bakery on the corner, where a small cluster of folks huddled around a decorative window display. Overhead, twinkling icicle lights still clung to storefront awnings, a reminder that the festival's spirit lingered.

"Mr. Benjamin, hey! I saw the crowds outside the B&B last week. Never seen so many tourists in one place before. Good for you."

Benjamin turned to find Mr. Kurt striding toward him, bundled in a flowing coat and a long scarf. The man exuded warmth despite the chill in the air, his voice carrying easily over the busy street.

Benjamin grinned, tipping his hat. "Thank you, Mr. Kurt."

They shook hands briefly, their breath condensing in the cold. Benjamin had always admired Kurt's easy, neighborly charm. They slowed as they approached the icy light pole near the Tax Office. Kurt crossed his arms, leveling a look at Benjamin. "That 'thank you' sounded a little reluctant."

Benjamin tittered, amused. "And what does that mean, sir?" He cast a glance up the street, watching pedestrians shuffle past, wrapped in scarves and gloves.

"I know your laugh." Kurt pointed at him knowingly, stepping closer. "It's firm and steady. But just now, that was a squeak. What's on your mind? Weren't you glad to have so many tourists at your business?" He smiled beneath a silver mustache. "I know I was buzzing when I saw folks packing into my cinema."

Benjamin chuckled, shaking his head. He didn't spend much time in conversation, but he and Kurt had developed a routine —a monthly lunch where they swapped business insights and town happenings. Benjamin had observed Kurt enough to read his moods, and evidently, the man had done the same.

"Mr. Kurt, I'm grateful for the six rooms that were booked last weekend," Benjamin admitted. "But you know how it is when you see room for improvement." He exhaled, rubbing his gloved hands together. "I don't understand why the B&B wasn't at full capacity like everywhere else."

Kurt tsk-tsked, shaking his head. "Ah, I see. The old businessman's shame is getting to you." He let out a hearty laugh. "Well, my friend, that probably means you need to get back to the drawing board." He glanced at his watch. "I have to go. See you soon, Benjamin."

Benjamin waved as Kurt hurried off. He continued down the street, hands in his coat pockets, his mind still churning over the issue. The festival had been wonderful for Sweetgum—lines outside the movie theater, new shops decorated with icicles and wreaths, street performers adding color and life. Yet for all that success, his B&B hadn't reaped the benefits he'd hoped for. A dozen thoughts vied for attention: was the place too traditional? Did potential guests crave something more modern, or more adventurous?

Dwelling on last weekend wouldn't change the fact that he had vacancies, but from a business standpoint, it was his job to figure out why. What had kept some tourists away? Was it the décor? The amenities? Had word gotten out that his B&B wasn't as modern as some of the newer inns?

He pictured the front parlor, which Ilene had once filled with warm, homey touches—quilts, antique lamps, old books on the shelves. Lately, though, he wondered if time had finally caught up with him. Younger visitors might crave spa-like luxuries or digital check-ins, things he'd never considered essential.

He crossed the street and stopped in front of the diner's glass doors. Maybe Kurt was right—maybe it was time to go back to the drawing board. But how did a man like Benjamin

Walters, who had built his business from the ground up and thrived for years, reinvent himself?

As he stood there thinking, a group of young people burst through the doors, laughing and talking animatedly about what they wanted for lunch. Their voices grew fainter as they disappeared inside, but something in their conversation caught Benjamin's attention.

The menu.

"Hmmm..."

The way they rattled off their options—dishes that hadn't been on the diner's menu a month ago—made him pause. The diner had adapted, changed things up. Was that the key? Should he ask folks inside for ideas? It was the creativity of Sweetgum's business owners that had turned the town into a tourist destination in the first place.

A slow, knowing smile spread across Benjamin's lips. Rochelle.

He tapped his gloved fingers against the door, that single thought steadying him. The memory of how she'd given up the diner to Malachi yet still seemed tethered to its evolving success. Her knack for adapting in subtle ways, never losing the essence of what made her place feel like home.

She may not have been the mastermind behind Sweetgum's transformation, but she had spent decades keeping her business afloat despite competition. Unlike him, she hadn't just contended with one hotel—she'd faced a revolving door of new eateries, snack shops, and bakeries all vying for customers. Yet, she had always found a way to stand out.

She's gotta have some answers.

Feeling lighter than he had all morning, Benjamin stepped into the diner and made his way to his usual table—the circular one smack in the middle of the building. He settled into the chair, rubbing his hands together, his gaze scanning the room until it landed on Rochelle.

His heart gave a faint jolt, recalling the bracelet he'd gifted her on Christmas Eve. The memory still brought a quiet warmth. Yes. This could work.

The only question now was: Would Rochelle be willing to help?

CHAPTER FIVE

"And I don't want you anywhere near any of these tables with a notepad." Malachi's grip on Rochelle's arms was firm yet playful, his touch more of a secure embrace than an actual restraint.

"Oh, is that so?" Rochelle arched a brow, her lips curving into a smirk. "And who exactly put you in charge of what I do or don't do in my retirement?"

Malachi gave her a knowing look before gently but persistently nudging her toward the counter. Rochelle dug in her heels, but the boy had grown strong over the years. Probably all that weightlifting he did before bed. It never failed to amaze her how much he had changed—how much he had grown. Time had a funny way of sneaking up on people.

Customers watched the spectacle unfold, their poorly concealed amusement flickering in smirks and barely stifled chuckles. She must have been quite the sight—Sweetgum's hotshot diner's new owner physically maneuvering its former proprietor away from work like a mischievous child being redirected.

With an exasperated sigh, Rochelle freed herself from

Malachi's grasp, smoothing out the wrinkles he had left on her cardigan. "You rumpled my clothes, Malachi." She ran a palm over the fabric, then lifted her chin. "I don't see why you're so dead set against me lending a hand. I picked one day—one—to come in and help out. Every other day, I do retirement things. That seems like a fair compromise to me."

Malachi folded his arms, tilting his head slightly as he pinned her with a pointed look. "And exactly how does that argument help your case? Today is Tuesday, not Wednesday." His voice nearly got lost in the chime of the doorbell and the buzz of lunchtime chatter. "Last I checked, you told me you were spending the afternoon with Mrs. Zhang. Was that a lie?"

Rochelle scoffed, tossing an empty notepad onto the counter. "Now, why would I lie to you?"

The tinkle of the old-fashioned chimes above the diner door announced a new customer, their melodic sound a familiar comfort.

"I am here to check in on my busybody buddy," came Mei's voice as she waltzed through the door, leading a line of new customers inside. Her red frock billowed like a flame, vibrant against the muted tones of the diner. "Are you done finding things to do? Can we have lunch?"

Malachi's expression flattened as he turned to them both. "Wait. You told Mrs. Zhang to meet you here? As in, you're having lunch here?"

Rochelle grinned, tapping her temple. "Where else would we eat? Isn't this the hottest place on the block?"

Malachi dragged a hand down his face with a long sigh. "Oh, Aunt Rochelle. One day, you will learn to let go." Despite his weariness, he flashed her a smile before disappearing behind the counter.

Mei adjusted the rope-like belt of her dress, cinching it at the waist. "He's right, you know." She guided Rochelle toward a booth by the window, away from the lunchtime crowd. "You need to let the boy take over."

"Oh, don't you start." Rochelle slid into the seat across from her. "I have let him take over. Coming in to help part-time isn't being overbearing. It's balance." She exhaled and placed her arms on the table, her fingers tracing invisible circles on the polished red surface. "This transition is hard for folks like me."

Mei studied her for a beat before reaching across the table to squeeze her wrist. "I understand, Rochelle, but I don't think throwing yourself back into what you just retired from is the answer." She let out a light laugh. "You, my friend, have to learn how to sit still."

Rochelle wrinkled her nose. "I guess so." She drummed her fingers against the table before reaching for the laminated menu. "So, what do you feel like ordering? I'm craving some of that tomato soup."

Mei flipped open her own menu, humming in thought. "Still deciding." Then, without missing a beat, she smirked. "Had any interesting meetings lately?" Her voice turned syrupy sweet. "At that little Christmas party, you looked real cozy with a certain someone you insist is just a nice man."

Rochelle rolled her eyes. "Oh, for heaven's sake."

This conversation was becoming Mei's favorite pastime. If they weren't matchmaking for the younger generation, Mei was pestering her about Benjamin. It had become the woman's personal mission to make something out of nothing.

"Now you," Rochelle pointed at her, "you need to behave yourself. Whatever happened with Mr. Benjamin that night was nothing but friendly gestures."

Mei gasped, clutching her chest dramatically. "Friendly gestures? Rochelle! The way you're holding it in, it's like someone holding in gas in a crowded room." She leaned in. "It's been weeks, woman. Spill it."

Rochelle waved her off, chuckling. "I already told you, Mei. Nothing happened."

"But you left out the good details." Mei's eyes gleamed with mischief. "You're holding back."

Rochelle shook her head. "If I let myself dwell on little things too much, I might start getting ideas. And you will certainly be no help in keeping me grounded."

Mei gasped again, this time in offense. "Do you think it's funny that I care?"

Rochelle smirked. "No, I just thought of something completely impossible."

"What?"

"I've outgrown the ability to have my heart broken."

Mei groaned. "Oh, please."

Just then, a shadow fell over their table.

Both women turned, and Rochelle's breath caught.

There he was.

Benjamin Walters, standing tall in a crisp blue sweater and even crisper jeans. He looked freshly put together, his presence warm and steady, a quiet confidence radiating from him.

"Benjamin." Rochelle recovered quickly, though something in her pulse had the nerve to skip. "Didn't expect to see you here."

Mei hummed smugly, sipping her water.

Benjamin folded his hands in front of him, his deep voice as smooth as butter. "I actually came to see you, Ms. Rochelle." He turned to Mei. "If that's alright with your lunch date here."

Mei grinned. "Oh, take her. She's yours." She waved them off. "You two enjoy."

Rochelle sent her a pointed look before following Benjamin away from the booth. He led her toward the quieter back area, near a small Christmas tree pop-up display by the hallway.

Benjamin clasped his hands. "Before I lay this out, how are you?"

Rochelle smiled. "Always good. You know what I always say?"

His lips twitched. "That a person makes the day bad or good."

She blinked. "Well, would you look at that? You do listen."

Benjamin chuckled. "I try."

Then, his tone shifted, more serious now. "Rochelle, I have a proposal."

Her pulse kicked up a notch.

"You ran this diner for decades, made it a staple despite the competition," he said. "I need your expertise. My B&B did fine during the festival, but not great. I want to take it from good to thriving—and I think you can help me get there."

Rochelle exhaled, something settling inside her. Of all things, she hadn't expected this. What the perfect cure for her retirement.

She tilted her head, curiosity dancing in her eyes. "Benjamin, what exactly are you looking for? My days of wearing an apron for the diner are behind me—but if you need a consultant, or maybe just some fresh eyes on the B&B…"

Benjamin nodded. "Consultant, partner in crime—whatever word suits you. I've noticed how you adapt to new trends without losing what makes a place feel like home. I need that. I need someone who's got the experience to see what's missing." He ran a hand over his jaw. "I wouldn't ask if I didn't believe you could make a real difference."

Something about his earnestness nudged Rochelle's heart. "You sure about that?" She arched an eyebrow. "I just got done telling Malachi how I'm trying to back off from butting my nose in."

Benjamin's eyes crinkled in a faint smile. "You're not butting in if you're invited. And I'm inviting you. Officially." He hesitated, searching her face. "I need your wisdom, Ms. Rochelle. When I first opened the B&B, it was me and Ilene. We poured everything we had into it. But times have changed, and I can't figure out how to shift with them."

Rochelle's gaze softened at the mention of Ilene. She recalled the shy warmth in Benjamin's eyes whenever he talked about his wife. "I remember how proud you both were when it first opened," Rochelle murmured. "Look, if you believe I can help, then I won't turn you down. But I need details. Are you thinking I'll pop by once a week with a checklist? Or do you want me digging in every day, rebranding the place entirely?"

Benjamin's throat bobbed. "I want you as involved as you can be. I've got some ideas for new packages, maybe a way to cater to couples. But I don't know if that'll fly. You know how to read what people want—and how to give it to them without losing authenticity." He released a slow breath. "Truth is, I'd rather not do a complete overhaul. I still want my B&B to feel like home. But it needs a spark."

Rochelle studied him in silence. The last few months of retirement had left her feeling restless, teetering between relief at having time to herself and a strange yearning for the bustle she'd once thrived in. This offer—this chance to nurture another business—felt like the perfect middle ground.

She grinned. "Honey, count me in."

Benjamin's expression lit up. "Are you sure? I don't want to drag you into something that might end up being another full-time job."

Rochelle laughed softly. "Boy, if I didn't want a challenge, I'd be at home right now reading my romance novels, sipping tea, and complaining about how I miss the diner. Truth is, I'm itching to do something worthwhile." She paused, tilting her head. "But I'll warn you—I'm opinionated, and I won't sugarcoat it if I think something's not going to work."

Benjamin chuckled. "That's exactly what I need. No sugar-coating."

They stood there for a moment, a shared excitement flickering between them like static electricity. Rochelle felt a familiar spark welling up in her—the same one she used to feel when brainstorming new menus or reorganizing the diner's layout. She'd missed that blend of innovation and intuition.

"Well," she finally said, crossing her arms in a playful show of confidence, "what's our first step?"

Benjamin exhaled in relief. "Maybe we brainstorm over coffee? Unless you've eaten."

Rochelle nodded toward the booth. "I was about to order lunch with Mei. I'm sure she won't mind me switching seats for a bit. Besides," she added wryly, "if she does, she'll just talk louder about you until the whole diner's overheard her commentary anyway."

Benjamin gave a warm laugh. "I like that idea. Let's talk details. I'll buy you lunch."

With a small smile, Rochelle placed a hand lightly on his arm. "It's a deal. Thank you, Benjamin—really."

He covered her hand with his. "The pleasure is all mine. Now, let's see what this place is serving up today."

Together, they wandered back toward the main part of the diner, side by side like old confidants on the verge of a brand-new adventure.

CHAPTER SIX

Benjamin couldn't recall the last time he'd genuinely sought anyone else's opinion on his business—let alone the opinion of someone he secretly admired. When he and Ilene had first opened the B&B all those years ago, it felt like it was simply their vision, their rules, and their combined sensibilities that would carry them to success. After Ilene's passing, Benjamin kept operating by habit and memory, trusting the routines he and his wife had established. But something in the air had shifted lately—maybe the energy of a changing Sweetgum, or maybe the pang of wanting companionship again. Whatever the cause, it was enough to nudge him out of that solitary mindset.

He found himself smoothing a plump throw pillow on the lobby's plush armchair, anxiously waiting for Rochelle to arrive. Light from the oversized windows spilled across the polished hardwood floor, illuminating the delicate grain in the wood. He inhaled slowly, picking up faint traces of lavender from a diffuser in the corner. A new housekeeper had insisted on those floral scents; the guests seemed to love them, and Benjamin decided it was a small, simple way to embrace change.

Still, his nerves hummed like a taut wire. Rochelle was coming by to help him brainstorm how to revitalize the B&B. And this wasn't just any adviser—this was Rochelle, the same woman who had lit up his holiday party and who had, unknowingly, begun to light up corners of his heart he thought were shut for good.

As he repositioned the pillow for the third time, a sudden gust of wind rattled the front door. A swirl of cold air drifted in, sending goosebumps pricking along his forearms. The older wooden frame of the entrance always seemed to creak in protest during winter, as though the building itself was complaining about the chill.

One of his junior staff, a shy college student named Ari, peeked in from the side hallway. "Sir, Ms. Rochelle is here," Ari said, voice wavering with excitement. Even they seemed curious about this formidable, warm-hearted woman who used to run the busiest diner in town.

Benjamin set the pillow aside and straightened his sweater. "Thank you, Ari. Let her in, please."

With that, Rochelle appeared, stepping through the door with a gently exhaled sigh. She looked wonderfully cozy wrapped in a thick, cream-colored sweater that highlighted her brown skin. A swirl of winter air followed her in, tugging at the loose hairs around her temples. Despite the cold, her cheeks glowed with vitality. She pressed her lips together in a shy smile as soon as she spotted him.

He caught the subtle scent of vanilla and something sweet—brown sugar, perhaps—lingering around her. The aroma made him want to draw closer, if only to enjoy that gentle warmth.

"Morning," he said, injecting cheer into his voice despite the sudden dryness in his throat. "You made it just in time. Another fifteen minutes, and you'd have had to wade through snow drifts to get here."

Rochelle let out a small laugh. "Well, I wasn't about to let a little cold get in the way of seeing your B&B in daylight. I've heard enough about it; now I want to get a real look."

Benjamin offered a polite nod, trying to contain his growing smile. "I appreciate your enthusiasm." He stepped forward, noticing how she rubbed her hands together for warmth. "You cold?"

She gave a quick shrug and a teasing half-smile. "I'm thawing out. You know how it is—no matter how thick the coat, winter manages to crawl under it sometimes."

"Here." He reached for the door behind her, easing it shut against a fresh gust of wind. The latch clicked, sealing them off from the swirl of snow outside. "We'll warm you up inside."

They took a few steps deeper into the lobby, letting the overhead chandelier's glow wash over them. Even in the quieter winter months, the B&B's lobby had a welcoming charm—slate-blue walls with white wainscoting, old photographs of Sweetgum in its early days, and an antique oak reception desk that Ilene had chosen herself. It creaked softly whenever someone leaned against it, and for a moment, Benjamin's chest tightened with nostalgia.

Rochelle's gaze roamed appreciatively over the décor. "It's got the feel of a home," she said, eyes lingering on the framed pictures of previous guests laughing and holding mugs of cocoa. "I can see why people love staying here. There's something personal about it all."

His heart swelled. Hearing Rochelle compliment the place he and Ilene had built felt like a gentle validation. "That's exactly what we aimed for," he said softly. "Ilene used to say she wanted everyone to walk in and think, 'Ah, I'm home.'"

Rochelle's expression softened. She reached out and gave his arm a brief, comforting squeeze. Her touch was warm, reassuring—so simple, yet it sent a current of awareness humming through his veins.

He cleared his throat to keep his composure. "Let me show

you around. We'll start with the ground floor and work our way up."

She nodded, following close behind. As they traversed the lobby, he pointed out the small library nook tucked beside the curved staircase—lined with books on local history, romance novels (a guilty favorite for many guests), and a few travel guides. The broad staircase swept in a gentle curve to the upper floors, its rail gleaming from regular polishing. On the right side of the lobby sat a pair of wide French doors, which were shut tight to keep out the draft but opened onto a patio in warmer months.

They came to a halt outside the dining room. Benjamin pushed the door open, revealing a quaint space set with tables with white linens. A large fireplace dominated one wall, its stone mantel displaying seasonal decorations—currently, a scattering of pinecones and winter berries. A few guests who had lingered after breakfast glanced up, offered polite nods, then returned to their conversation.

Rochelle's eyes brightened. "I can imagine this place on a busy weekend—chatter drifting between the tables, coffee cups clinking, that fireplace blazing away."

Benjamin leaned against the doorframe, remembering how lively it used to get. "During the holidays, it's even more festive. I put up garlands, some fairy lights around the mantel—just enough to keep the holiday spirit alive without overwhelming the space."

Rochelle's gaze drifted along the mantel, then dropped to the plush rug near the fireplace. "You could do couples' dinners in here," she suggested, a spark of excitement in her voice. "Imagine candlelit evenings with special pairings—like a set menu with dessert for two." She cast him a sidelong glance. "Or maybe host small vow renewal ceremonies if the couples are more mature. Give them a private, cozy atmosphere."

The idea warmed him. "I like that," he said, his tone

measured but intrigued. He'd never thought to use the dining room for vow renewals, and he could already see how the flickering firelight might bounce off the champagne glasses. "You see everything through such a creative lens."

She smiled. "I've been known to help set up a wedding or two in my day, so I can't help seeing possibilities."

He motioned for her to follow him out. "Speaking of possibilities, let's head upstairs, and I'll show you a few of the guest rooms."

They made their way back into the lobby and up the main staircase. Each step creaked faintly, reminding Benjamin of how Ilene used to joke that the old house was gossiping about its occupants. The second-floor landing branched off into a long hallway, framed by rich burgundy carpeting. Benjamin pointed out three guest rooms—one done in soft blues, another in gentle pastels, and the last in earth tones with a large bay window overlooking the back garden.

Rochelle stepped into the earth-toned room, immediately pausing at the window. Thin winter light filtered through the glass, illuminating faint swirling snow on the other side. "I love this view," she whispered, pressing a palm to the cool glass. "Even in winter, it's so peaceful. People pay top dollar for a sense of tranquility like this."

Benjamin joined her, standing a careful distance away so as not to intrude on her personal space. He studied the reflection of her face in the window—her eyes bright with thoughtful consideration. "In the spring, it's breathtaking. Flowers, vines… The garden practically explodes with color."

She turned, her gaze locking with his. "Maybe we can emphasize that in the marketing—like a highlight of the property. 'Wake up to a painter's palette of blooms,' or something like that."

He chuckled, feeling a gentle swell of hope. "You really

believe people will come just for a glimpse of some roses and irises?"

She arched a brow. "If you package it right—and keep the romance going—absolutely. You've got a lot to offer here, Benjamin. Sometimes you just need to show it in the right light."

Her words resonated, and he felt the faint stir of an unfamiliar excitement—a kind of optimism he hadn't felt since Ilene was alive. "We can do that."

They moved on to the next hallway, strolling side by side. Their footsteps were hushed by the runner carpet, and Benjamin noticed how comfortable he felt walking like this. Rochelle seemed at ease too, though every now and then, he spotted a flicker of something thoughtful behind her eyes, as if the wheels in her head were constantly turning.

At the end of the corridor, they descended a smaller, older staircase that led to the ground floor's rear exit—a set of double doors with frosted glass. A cold draft leaked through the tiny gaps, but Rochelle pressed forward, peering outside.

"All right," she declared, rubbing her gloved hands together. "Ready to brave the cold?"

Benjamin reached around to unhook a spare coat from the rack. "It's biting out there," he warned. He slipped the coat gently over her shoulders. "This will help."

She glanced up in a flicker of surprise, then offered a grateful smile. "Thank you."

They stepped outside into the swirl of midmorning snow. The sky hovered in a somber gray, but there was a stark beauty in how the bare tree branches contrasted with the pristine white. Rochelle paused on the stone patio, exhaling a visible breath. The cold nipped at her cheeks, turning them a shade darker. Benjamin stayed close, almost protectively so.

Past a short walkway lay the greenhouse—a small, glass-sided structure that still shimmered with leftover icicles clinging to its edges. Snow had piled up at the greenhouse's foundation. Benjamin carefully cleared the step with his boot, then opened the squeaky door.

Inside, the temperature jumped. It wasn't balmy, but it was certainly warmer, thanks to the modest heating system tucked away in one corner. Rochelle visibly relaxed, letting out a content sigh. "Oh, this is lovely," she murmured.

She wandered deeper among rows of potted herbs and winter blooms. Benjamin could practically see her mind cataloging every detail—the arrangement of plants, the gentle condensation on the glass walls, the vibrant pops of green against the dull winter outside.

"This belonged to my wife," he said softly. The glass structure echoed the hush in his voice. "Ilene tended to the greenhouse year-round, using it as her personal project. We'd sometimes use the herbs she grew here for breakfast dishes." He let out a wistful laugh. "I remember her standing exactly where you are, fussing with those little pots of basil, determined to perfect her pesto recipe."

Rochelle brushed a hand gently over a row of young tomato plants. "It must be comforting to keep this going. A way to keep her memory alive."

Benjamin nodded, swallowing a sudden lump in his throat. "It is," he managed. "For a while, it felt too heavy to come in here alone. But over time, I realized staying away only robbed me of the good memories."

They shared a glance—her eyes reflecting empathy, his a quiet gratitude. Outside, wind whistled against the greenhouse, but in that moment, the hush felt safe, cocooned by glass and faint warmth.

Rochelle cleared her throat gently. "Couples would absolutely love this," she said. "A hidden greenhouse in the middle of winter? It's romantic, it's unique—makes for a memory they won't forget." She turned in place, arms drifting out as if envisioning it from every angle. "You could host small gatherings here. Or even let people pick fresh herbs to add to their dinner—like an interactive cooking experience for couples who want something different."

The corners of Benjamin's mouth lifted in a smile that felt unguarded. "I never even thought about that," he admitted. "I like the idea."

When she pivoted to face him again, he noticed how the overhead light caught the subtle silver threads at her temples, the lines near her eyes that only deepened when she smiled. There was no denying her grace, the calm confidence of a woman who had lived, loved, and still had so much more to give.

"So," Rochelle said, voice echoing softly among the plants, "we've got the romantic dining room, scenic guestrooms, a cozy lobby, and an enchanting greenhouse. I see a pattern, Benjamin. This place is practically tailor-made for love."

He let out a gentle laugh, the warmth in his tone matching her smile. "Maybe I just needed fresh eyes to see it."

She stepped closer—close enough for him to notice the flecks of color in her irises—and squeezed his forearm in a companionable gesture. "We'll make this B&B into a place folks talk about for years."

Benjamin's heart thrummed. "I believe we will," he said quietly.

They lingered for a moment longer among the plants, letting the hush speak for them. Then Rochelle gestured toward the door. "It's still cold outside, but I could go for a warm cup of coffee if you've got the time."

Benjamin grinned. "I've always got time for you, Ms. Rochelle."

Together, they headed back through the snowfall, leaving footprints side by side on the path. And Benjamin's chest felt a bit fuller.

CHAPTER SEVEN

ochelle could still feel the lingering winter chill on her cheeks by the time she and Benjamin got back inside. The moment they crossed the threshold, the comforting aroma of faint cinnamon and flickering fireplace embers washed over her. As they stepped through the lobby, Rochelle noticed a young couple in matching wool sweaters standing up from their seats near the fire. The pair exchanged a few whispered words before disappearing, hand in hand, up the staircase.

Watching them go stirred a gentle warmth in Rochelle's chest. Couples. That's exactly what this place could be full of, if things went right. Of course, she wasn't about to blurt that out again. After all, she was just a consultant here—though part of her was giddy at the thought of ushering in a new wave of romance to Benjamin's B&B.

Soon, she found herself alone in the cozy living room space, feeling the soft hush that descended whenever guests retreated to their rooms. The quiet was pleasant, wrapping her in a sense of calm. She thought back to Benjamin's offer to make her at home while he prepared coffee—an offer she was more than happy to accept.

Rochelle made her way over to a squat bookshelf, running a finger across the neat rows of paperbacks. She recognized the titles of some old classics and a few bestsellers. Her gaze floated up to the mantel, where delicate decorative pieces and a small family photo were arranged with care. In that photo, Benjamin stood proudly beside a smiling, dark-haired woman. Ilene, she realized—Benjamin's late wife. Rochelle lingered just a moment, thoughts flicking to how sweet and joyful they looked together. A subtle pang twinged in her chest, a mixture of empathy and something unnamed that she didn't want to examine too closely.

Turning away, she sank onto the couch. Its retro design was pure sixties—clean lines, bright upholstery, and cushions that sank just enough when she sat. The living room was otherwise a charming blend of old and new. Across from her stood a state-of-the-art TV, so sleek it looked almost out of place. She picked up the remote, tested out a few buttons, then gave a little snort of amusement when the screen flashed through multiple menus she didn't recognize.

With a grin, she settled on a rerun of a cozy mystery show. Its familiar theme music hummed through the living room at a gentle volume. As she relaxed into the cushions, Rochelle appreciated the subtle hum of the furnace kicking on, sending warm air drifting through the vents. Truth be told, she was still thawing out from the trip outside to see the greenhouse. A delicate ache clung to her fingertips—a reminder of just how cold it had been.

Her eyes drifted to the flames dancing in the fireplace. The gentle pop and crackle reminded her of nights from her diner days, when she'd come home after a long shift, fix a cup of herbal tea, and curl up by her own fireplace to chase away the day's fatigue. The memory made her smile, though it also carried a note of nostalgia for that busier time in her life. No matter how comfortable retirement was supposed to be, a part of her still craved that sense of purpose.

A moment later, soft footsteps approached behind the couch.

"Here you are, Ms. Rochelle," came Benjamin's voice, low and smooth.

She glanced over her shoulder and smiled, taking the dark red mug he offered. Steam curled upward, carrying the rich scent of freshly brewed coffee. Even as she savored that aroma, she noticed how Benjamin lingered a moment—almost like he was making sure she was truly comfortable.

"Hope you made it strong," she teased, gently cradling the mug in her hands. The heat warmed her palms in an instant. "I'm gonna need it if we're gonna talk shop."

Benjamin chuckled softly, rounding the couch to settle beside her. The cushion dipped under his weight. "I made it just how you like," he said, his gaze flicking briefly to the TV. "No complaints, I hope?"

She lifted the mug for a quick sip, smiling at the pleasantly bitter taste. "We'll see," she answered, aiming for playful. "I reserve the right to change my mind if it's not perfect."

He folded his hands in his lap, posture noticeably stiff. "I've been bracing myself for your critique ever since you arrived," he admitted, a little laugh catching in his throat. "You've got an eye for detail—I just want to make this place shine. Don't hold back."

Rochelle swallowed another mouthful of coffee, letting the warmth bloom across her chest. She set the mug on the coffee table, her brow creasing in mild concern. "Benjamin, you don't have to be so hard on yourself. Your place is wonderful. Really." She swept a hand around, taking in the tasteful blend of mid-century furniture, modern electronics, and old-fashioned charm. "It's homey, but not stuffy. Nostalgic, yet modern enough to make folks feel like they're not missing out on today's comforts. It's… well, it's special."

Benjamin's lips curved in a slow, self-conscious smile. He exhaled, shoulders sagging in relief. "Thank you for saying that. I guess I worry I'm behind the times, especially with all these new businesses cropping up around town."

She tilted her head, casting a thoughtful glance at the fireplace. "Yes, there are new places—a handful of fancy inns and modern rentals—but they don't have your authenticity." Turning to face him, she lifted a finger. "However, I noticed something about your B&B that could be your strongest selling point."

Leaning forward, Benjamin rested his elbows on his knees. "I'm listening."

"It's romantic." The word slipped out with more enthusiasm than she intended. Rochelle found her cheeks warming. "I mean… yes, it's great for families or lone travelers, but the place practically breathes warmth for couples. From that cozy fire over there to the greenhouse, from the intimate dining area to the scenic rooms upstairs… It feels like stepping into one of those classic love stories. You know, the kind where two people meet under unexpected circumstances and bond over shared cups of hot cocoa."

Benjamin studied her, an intrigued flicker in his dark eyes. "Romantic," he repeated. "I never consciously aimed for that, but I can see where you're coming from."

Rochelle shrugged, leaning back against the couch cushions. "It's the perfect environment to lean into. Folks of all ages crave a warm, welcoming place to reconnect—or maybe even meet someone new. If you emphasize the romance factor—couple's getaways, special dinners, vow renewals—you might tap into an entire market you've never targeted before."

For a moment, Benjamin was quiet. He rubbed his chin as though weighing her words, and Rochelle felt a brief flash of worry that she might have gone too far. Then, he let out a low chuckle. "That sounds… exciting, actually," he said with an air of relief. "I guess there's nothing wrong with reminding people that love can still bloom at any stage in life."

Delighted, Rochelle clapped her hands softly. "Exactly. Welcome couples of all ages—newlyweds, longtime partners celebrating anniversaries, or maybe even people hoping to find someone special in a quiet, inspiring space."

Her excitement bubbled over, and she reached again for her coffee mug, letting the aroma ground her. "I can already picture the marketing ideas. We can show the greenhouse as a highlight, maybe mention the fireplace as the perfect setting for sipping mulled wine on a winter night…"

Benjamin chuckled, his entire demeanor more open now. "I'm sold. Seems I hired the right consultant."

At that, Rochelle's cheeks flushed. She wasn't entirely sure why, but hearing him say she was "the right consultant" flooded her with a warm sense of pride. "I'm no expert in fancy marketing," she cautioned, "but I know people, and I know how to make them feel at home. You've got the base—now we'll just shape it into something that stands out."

His gaze drifted to the low table behind the couch, where an older photo of Ilene rested in a delicate silver frame. For a second, Rochelle thought she spotted a flicker of sadness in his eyes. He breathed in deeply and squared his shoulders. "I appreciate you, Rochelle. More than I can say."

She reached over and patted his hand, offering a gentle squeeze before letting go. "Don't you worry. Once I get my hands on things, we'll have people flocking here for that sweet, small-town romance vibe."

"Small-town romance vibe," he echoed, a playful note in his voice. "Well, I can't think of anyone who understands that vibe better than you, Ms. Rochelle."

Their eyes met for a moment. The fire popped in the hearth,

throwing sparks of orange light across the room. Rochelle felt her heart give a funny little stutter. She distracted herself with another sip of coffee.

"So… what's our next step?" Benjamin asked, voice quieter now. "I'd guess we'll need some sort of plan, maybe a timeline?"

Rochelle set her mug down, crossing one ankle over the other. "I'll whip up a quick marketing outline, focusing on the romance angle. Then we can talk about sprucing up the website —photos, maybe a short video tour. If we time it right, we can launch this new 'romance retreat' idea just before Valentine's Day or early spring, when the garden starts waking up."

Benjamin nodded thoughtfully, a faint grin tugging at the corner of his lips. "Sounds good. This is… a lot to take in, but it feels right."

"It does," Rochelle agreed softly. "We can do as much or as little as you're comfortable with. Baby steps, if that's easier."

He lifted a hand, palm up. "Or big leaps. I'm not opposed to diving in headfirst if it means this place flourishes."

Rochelle reached across the small space between them, giving his hand another quick press. She felt the steady warmth of his skin beneath her fingertips. "I like the sound of that."

For a while, they lapsed into companionable silence. The old mystery show on TV droned on, flickering scenes of amateur sleuths and suspicious neighbors, while the crackling embers in the fireplace punctuated the hush. Outside the window, Rochelle could see flurries of snow dancing against the twilight sky, reminding her it was still winter—even if inside, the talk of new beginnings felt like a slow bud of spring.

Eventually, Rochelle cleared her throat, the huskiness of the warm room tugging her toward a drowsy comfort. "I should probably head home soon," she said, though she made no move to stand just yet.

Benjamin nodded, adjusting his position on the couch. "I'll

walk you out. And, Rochelle"—his voice dipped a fraction—"thank you again. For everything."

She managed a small, genuine smile. "Of course. Let's make some magic happen here."

As he turned off the TV, Rochelle's mind drifted to the day's discoveries: a greenhouse rich with Ilene's memory, a cozy living room perfect for couples, and the gentle nudge that told her, though life had changed many times over, there was still room for something new to bloom. Not just for Benjamin's B&B, but perhaps… for her, too.

CHAPTER EIGHT

Benjamin absently twirled a half-eaten breadstick between his fingers, leaning back in the wooden dining chair as he watched Rochelle across the table. She had all but demolished her bowl of tomato-basil soup, spoon scraping the bottom in search of one last taste. He grinned. He'd long known Rochelle appreciated good food—she'd owned a diner, after all—but seeing her relish every spoonful made him appreciate her vitality in a new light.

When she finally set her spoon down, her cheeks were flushed with satisfaction. A trickle of sunlight from the nearby window caught in her hair, highlighting her salt and pepper strands. It was midafternoon, and the winter sun slanted in at a low angle, drenching the kitchen in a warm, honey-toned glow. Outside, a swirl of frost still clung to the corners of the windowpanes. Inside, though, the air felt welcoming—almost intimate.

Benjamin took another bite of his breadstick before turning back to Rochelle, whose laptop was perched on the edge of the table. Her eyes gleamed with a mix of anticipation and pride as she tapped a key, bringing up a fresh slide in the PowerPoint she'd been presenting. He could see the reflection of bright graphics dance across her face.

"Alright," she began, her voice lightly teasing as she cleared her throat. "You've seen the brainstorming slides, the color palettes, and the décor suggestions. Now, the slogan took me a while to come up with." She clicked another button, and the final slide bloomed onto the screen. "But I think it'll catch people's attention."

Benjamin leaned forward, discarding the remaining bread-stick into its basket. He squinted at the bold text:

"Find love after you sleep: Your match awaits at the Sweetgum Meadows B&B."

He let the words roll around in his head, speaking them aloud in a subdued murmur. "Find love after you sleep... your match awaits..." He rubbed his chin, mulling it over. The concept was certainly unique—something that might spark curiosity in young singles or older folks looking for a second shot at romance. Though the phrase was whimsical, it carried an underlying promise that felt oddly hopeful.

He glanced at Rochelle, whose face practically glowed with excitement. Her hands hovered above the laptop keys, waiting for his reaction. "That's really catchy," he finally said, offering a slow nod. "Did you come up with it all by yourself?"

Rochelle's grin widened, and she flipped a stray curl away from her face. "I sure did," she replied, tapping a manicured nail on the screen. "And I worked on this entire slideshow on my own. I might've had a smidgen of help with the tech stuff, but everything else—like these photos and the colors—was my brainchild."

He cocked his head to the side, letting his gaze linger on the pale reds and earthy browns she'd chosen as accent colors. They reminded him of terra-cotta pots and rose petals, a gentle warmth that hinted at romance without screaming hearts-and-flowers cliché. "The theme," he said slowly, "it's… interesting. Very imaginative. And it looks great."

She seemed to sense his hesitation. "But…?" She raised an eyebrow, bracing herself.

Benjamin dipped his breadstick into the last of his tomato soup. "But," he echoed, glancing at the PowerPoint, "it almost feels fairytale-like. I don't mean that in a bad way," he added quickly, lifting a hand. The last thing he wanted was to deflate her enthusiasm. "I mean it's so out of the box—it reminds me of the storybook romances folks dream about."

Rochelle's brow furrowed, and she slowly closed the laptop a few inches. "Fairytale-like, huh? Is that code for 'unrealistic'?"

Benjamin cursed himself for stumbling. "No—really, I only meant it's fresh. People will probably love it, especially younger folks. But we shouldn't forget couples who are already established or older singles who might not relate to something too whimsical."

He reached for his coffee mug, needing a sip to compose himself. "If it's primarily for singles, that's fine. Just be prepared for some customers who might also want a quieter, more traditional couple's retreat."

Rochelle nodded, though her shoulders relaxed a bit. "Actually, I did think about that," she said, tapping the laptop. "But then it occurred to me—there are loads of folks out there searching for love, at all different ages. A place like this could bring them together. Isn't that what people on online dating sites are hoping for—some kind of real connection? We could offer a weekend-long 'live version,' in a place that already feels romantic."

Benjamin mulled over the notion, picturing a full house at the B&B with guests mingling, attending little workshops or coffee socials, hoping to meet someone special in person. The idea carried a spark of excitement. "It's bold," he admitted, glancing at the window. Outside, flecks of snow glistened in the afternoon sunshine, a reminder that the world was still locked in winter's embrace. "Seeing it all unfold could be... well, it could be invigorating."

A pause settled between them, not at all uneasy. Benjamin's mind churned with the possibilities of her proposal, while Rochelle watched him with a curious tilt of her head. Finally, he let out a slow breath and smiled. "I think I'm ready to officially bring you on board as my marketing consultant, Ms. Rochelle. Let's do this."

She set the laptop aside with a flourish. "Oh, don't worry," she teased, "let me finish my soup before I sign anything." She nabbed one last spoonful, making a show of savoring it. "Priorities, Benjamin."

He chuckled, taking a sip of his coffee. The roasted aroma soothed him, grounding him in the moment. "Alright, I like the sound of that." He let his gaze wander around the bright kitchen, noticing how the golden sunlight caught the faint swirl of steam rising from Rochelle's soup bowl. He couldn't remember the last time discussing business had felt this... lively.

Memories drifted to the surface of his mind—memories of when he and Ilene had first opened the B&B, the starry-eyed excitement that propelled them through countless late nights of planning. It had been a shared dream, one that kept him going even after she passed. Yet, as time slipped by, some of that initial thrill had faded, replaced by day-to-day maintenance. Now, with Rochelle's new angle, it felt like a gust of fresh air blowing through a stuffy window.

"You know," he said softly, setting down his mug, "the last time I felt this excited about the B&B was right when we opened. Ilene and I poured our hearts into it." His eyes flicked to a small painting on the wall—a lavender field that Ilene had picked out because it reminded her of restful vacations in the French countryside. "Every room, every piece of décor—she had a hand in it."

Rochelle followed his gaze, then glanced around. "Did she have a say in this kitchen, too?" She jerked her chin toward the fridge, covered in multicolored magnets. Some spelled out random words; others were just decorative. "Because that's definitely a unique look."

A low laugh rumbled in his throat. "She had a sense of fun, that's for sure. We both liked leaving silly messages for each other. She called it 'the fridge of surprises.'"

Rochelle's lips curved into a gentle smile. "Well, that sense of fun is still here, even if she isn't. I think she'd be thrilled to know you're breathing new life into this place."

Benjamin felt a sudden tightness in his chest—a mix of longing for Ilene and gratitude for Rochelle's understanding. "She told me, toward the end, to do whatever I wanted with the B&B. That includes carrying on or selling it, or… well, anything. I've tried to preserve what she loved, but also to keep moving forward."

Rochelle reached across the table, resting her fingertips on the back of his hand. The gesture was soft, warm—an unspoken show of solidarity. "Grief is tricky," she said gently. "But so is guilt when you move forward. It's like you're scared to change anything because you don't want to lose what's left of someone's memory."

Benjamin nodded, turning his hand to give her fingers a light squeeze. "Exactly. I've had to learn that it's possible to honor someone's legacy without chaining yourself to it." He paused, letting out a contemplative sigh. "You mentioned your sister before—Malachi's mother. Is it the same for you?"

Her expression turned wistful. "In many ways, yes. After she passed, I kept thinking, 'What would she have wanted me to do?' But eventually I realized the best way to honor her was to keep living—to keep loving the people she loved and to find new joys of my own."

She slid her hand back, and they both turned their attention to the scattered dishes on the table. "Alright," she declared, clearing her throat, "enough heart-to-heart for one day. Let's do these dishes so I can say I contributed to the workload before I officially sign on as your marketing guru."

Benjamin stood with his plate, a light grin still curving his lips. "Fair enough." He grabbed a sponge, and as Rochelle came up beside him, her hand brushed his. A gentle spark fluttered through him at the contact—surprising and yet not unwelcome.

"Thanks," she murmured, stepping aside so he could start the water. "I'll let you handle your own sink."

He let out a soft laugh. "I appreciate that. But soon enough, you'll be so official around here that you'll own half the place."

She blinked in mock surprise. "Look at you, already offering me half your kingdom," she teased. "Slow down, Romeo."

Benjamin chuckled. "Just you wait until tomorrow," he said, his voice low, teasing. "I'm drafting up those consultant papers, and once you've signed them, I might just put you to work every day."

Rochelle's eyes sparkled with unspoken challenge. "Tomorrow it is, then."

He nodded, focusing on the steady rush of water filling the sink. Yet, as he scrubbed a soup bowl, he couldn't help glancing at Rochelle out of the corner of his eye. She stood beside him, wiping a plate with a clean dish towel, the soft lines of her face aglow with an energy he found undeniably comforting.

Yes, he thought, there was so much that could still bloom here—at his B&B, in his life, and perhaps even between them. He dared not name it just yet, but the thought was enough to send a ripple of anticipation through him. When Rochelle flashed him a bright smile, he found himself returning it with a sense of renewed hope, thinking, Tomorrow's going to be a good day.

CHAPTER NINE

The possibilities were endless with this new gig Rochelle had found herself in, and she couldn't wait to explore them all. These were her thoughts as she got dressed the following morning, fixing her hair in the mirror before pulling on a toasty jacket to head out.

Nothing felt better than eating out for breakfast. Though Rochelle found her own cooking superior to just about everyone else's, she still appreciated the times when meal prep wasn't a chore waiting for her.

She left her home with an appetite for Chinese breakfast and optimism burning at the center of her heart. Benjamin would sing her praises forever once she put the B&B on the map. They had discussed most of her plans over lunch, but there was still room for even more improvement.

As Rochelle walked down Main Street under the gray-blue sky, her thoughts wandered back to their conversation. *Need someone to sleep beside me at night...* She'd said it out loud. And flirtatiously, at that.

Why had she done that?

"Mornin', Rochelle," one of her church friends greeted her brightly while passing in the opposite direction.

Rochelle waved back, then stuffed her hands into her coat pockets, the fur-trimmed cuffs brushing against her wrists. The warmth of her jacket did little to shake the sudden cold sensation crawling down her back.

Had Benjamin thought she was being too forward? He had always been sweet, and Mei was convinced that he liked her, but Rochelle shouldn't have behaved that way after hearing about his wife. Sure, he had made it clear that she had *wanted* him to move on, but was it right?

Or was her mind just trying to justify why she *shouldn't* put herself out there?

She scoffed, slowing in front of Mei's restaurant. The sign on the glass door clearly read *Closed,* but that didn't apply to her. *At my age, I don't have time to get caught up in love and its confusion.* Like she kept telling herself—her time had passed.

After calling Mei to confirm she was inside, Rochelle admired the red lanterns swaying gently from the ceiling. She had always liked the ambiance they brought.

The door scraped open, and Mei greeted her with a knowing smile. "Come inside, Rochelle. I just got the food off the fire."

Moments later, they sat face-to-face at a booth near the window. Mr. Zhang was wiping down the counters, setting up for the day. The restaurant felt eerie without its usual crowd, the absence of chattering customers making the space feel almost too large. The sun had yet to fully rise, casting a dim glow through the windows.

But meeting at the crack of dawn on random Thursdays was what made their friendship *real.*

"I hope you like my new wonton recipe." Mei held up a dumpling between her chopsticks and took a bite, savoring it.

Rochelle had once attempted using chopsticks at Mei's restaurant but had ended up dropping food in her lap and nearly lodging a stick in her throat. So now, she stuck to forks. "It's great," she said after swallowing a wonton. "Keep this up, and you might be as good as me one day when it comes to cooking."

Mei rolled her eyes. "We *all* know I already passed you. Haven't seen you beat me at Chinese cuisine yet. Meanwhile, I can make *all* the American food you whip up in that diner." She winked before laughing. "Anyway, it's good to see you when no one is around. Sometimes us old girls need time all to ourselves."

"Tell me about it. When we eat out and there are yapping kids around, it can get tiring." Rochelle picked up her glass of orange juice. "But as much as they drain energy, they can replenish it, too." She smirked. "And you'd better get used to having even more little ones around, since your son is definitely going to have a baby one day."

Mei blinked as if stunned. "I haven't heard that boy say anything about babies—at least, not lately." She rubbed her chin with her chopsticks. "But we'll cross that bridge when we get there." She raised her chin toward Rochelle. "*You'll* have to as well. We *both* know Malachi and Aimee are going to have sweet little ones someday. You're like a mother to him, so we'll be grandmas together."

Rochelle laughed at the thought. "Ah, look at us." She gestured to the empty restaurant. "Old and ready to say hello to the new."

"Ah, we're *not* that old." Mei's voice cut through Rochelle's brief moment of reflection. "In fact, we're only old if we *say* we are."

Rochelle chuckled. "How can I be old when I'm taking on a *whole* new job?"

"Oh yes!" Mei's face lit up. Rochelle had given her the details over the phone last night, but they had yet to discuss it in person.

"I got the job," Rochelle said proudly. "All I have to do is sign the papers, and Mama will be back to making businesses thrive!"

Mei laughed. "You just *can't* resist work, can you?" She took another bite. "When I retire, you *won't* see me digging up projects for myself."

"Please. Like you could *stand* the boredom of retirement." Rochelle waved her off. "I could tell Mr. Ben was a little iffy about the whole thing, but he's open. We'll see how it all plays out."

Mei placed her hands gently on the table, her expression turning mischievous. "How it all plays out." She took a slow sip of her coffee.

Rochelle sighed. "Mei..."

"I'd like to see it unfold. I've been *rooting* for you and Benjy since the day he started coming around the diner."

There she *goes* again. Rochelle threw her head back with a laugh. "How many times do I have to say that me and that man are *nothing* but acquaintances?"

Mei arched a brow. "His love for you is more obvious than the color of the sky. You just refuse to see it because you *don't* want to hope too hard."

Rochelle felt her face heat. "I *don't* want to hope too hard?" Something about that didn't sit right. She wasn't a coward. "And who says that, huh?"

Mei tilted her head knowingly. "I don't understand how you can see who'd work well as a couple and *who'll* get married next, but you can't tell when a kind gentleman *wants* you in his life."

Rochelle stared at her, heart racing.

Mei leaned in. "It's alright to dream, Roche. Because sometimes, if you dream hard enough, they *come true.*"

Rochelle guffawed. "You *and* your fantasies. You're sweet, but this coconut has had it *up to here* with dating." She held her hand over her head. "I'm *old,* Mei."

Mei raised a finger. "Exactly. Old. Not *dead.*"

Rochelle let out a deep laugh but waved her hand dismissively. "My time has come and gone."

"Well..." Mei traced the rim of her cup. "Ben obviously thinks otherwise."

The restaurant would open soon. The *real* morning rush would begin.

And Rochelle still wasn't sure if Mei was talking nonsense— or saying the exact thing she needed to hear.

CHAPTER TEN

*W*ho knew one woman could sprout so many plans?

It was Benjamin and Rochelle's first official meeting as partners since she had finally signed her contract, and the woman was going wild.

"… I heard they have this amazing seat for just two people at the very back of the parlor that just *screams* romantic date. I've never seen any couples taking advantage of it, but who knows what could come out of such a great spot if we get that Rashad fella to spice it up."

She had hooked up a PowerPoint to his living room TV, flipping through slides with the confidence of a woman on a mission. They were once again on the B&B's highest floor—his private living space. Though she'd only been here once before, during last meeting's lunch date, Rochelle seemed right at home. She'd shrugged off her jacket upon entering and got right down to business.

Benjamin rubbed his beard, listening intently. Rochelle's PowerPoint was well made, filled with images of potential date ideas for their future patrons. At first, when she had mentioned marketing to singles, he had been confused. But now, with her thorough explanations, he understood exactly what she envisioned.

"But are you sure they'd be willing to do that? And not just Rashad. You mentioned partnering up with three other businesses. What if they're not interested in helping us place our couples on dates?" He leaned back, running a hand over his head. "And how are we so sure that the singles who come will actually like anyone else staying here at the same time?"

Rochelle tapped her laptop on the TV stand. "Did you *forget* slide seven? They'll be open to it because *they're* the ones signing up for the experience. If it doesn't work out, it doesn't. But if we try hard enough, I'm sure it will." She clicked back to the slide, the words bold and confident on the screen. "As long as people are compatible, things can work. And imagine having a romantic date at a dance studio."

Benjamin scratched his head as she skipped several slides to show off a photo of a couple smiling at a restaurant. "When did you even put all this together?"

"Last night." Rochelle smirked, bumping her hip against the TV stand. She looked spunky in her jeans and oversized sweater, a scarf tied neatly around her neck. "Don't let the whole thing hurt your head, Ben. If you open up your mind and *breathe in* the new ideas, I *know* you'll be even more on board than I am." She gave him her back to keep tinkering with her laptop. "Now, as I was saying..."

"Wait, wait, wait." Benjamin held up a hand, trying to keep up.

She finally paused and turned to him. "Yes?"

He scooted to the edge of his seat, the wood creaking beneath him. "You seem to think this whole matchmaking thing and all the dates will go perfectly well, but... what if some of the singles get into a heated argument? With so many people coming here looking for something special, misunderstandings are bound to happen. What do we do then?"

Rochelle clasped her hands and darted her eyes toward the kitchen. "We just need to set up policies. That, and hire extra security. But I doubt that'll happen a lot. Most folks know how to behave in a foreign place. They'd be scared of getting kicked out, just like in any other establishment."

She was convinced, but Benjamin wasn't sure he agreed. It could have been his spinning head or his reluctance toward change, but all of this seemed *big*. "And again, with the partnerships," he said. "Do you really think Roasted Beans Coffee and the others will go along with this?"

She frowned. "Don't laugh at my ideas." Rochelle crossed her arms. "Didn't you say you respected my outlook and innovation?"

Benjamin reeled back. "Rochelle, I..." He sighed. His words *had* come off the wrong way. "I didn't mean to offend you. It's just..." He gestured to the TV. "It's all so *big*. I never imagined expanding my business to the point of partnering with others."

Memories of the B&B's humble beginnings surfaced. Ilene welcoming visitors, Benjamin himself watering the plants, the two of them running things together. *Was he really ready for this?*

"The idea is so new that it's almost unfathomable to me," he admitted. "I apologize."

Rochelle's shoulders relaxed. She glanced at the slide on the screen. "I get that. I do. The B&B has been the quiet spot for decades here in Sweetgum. To completely revamp it and team up with other places is going to be new for *everyone*. But if you want to stay relevant and in people's minds..." She walked to the couch and perched on the arm. "You gotta be *bold, brave, and new*."

Her eyes sparkled with excitement, every inch of her believing in what they were doing.

Benjamin held the back of his head, mulling it over. His

main concern was whether the changes would bring chaos. They weren't guaranteeing that every single guest would find love, but what if expectations weren't met? What if Rochelle's matchmaking idea didn't work? The last thing he wanted was nasty reviews piling up.

"Ben? Why'd you go all quiet on me?" Rochelle ran her fingers through her afro before standing up. "Okay, look. It's *your* business. If you don't want us getting too involved with other businesses, I'll respect it."

Benjamin saw her face fall ever so slightly. He couldn't let that happen. "No. That's not it." He pointed at her. "I think the only way to *truly* know if your scheme will work is to *test* it." A grin tugged at his lips. "A trial run."

Rochelle's brows lifted. "Hey!" She clapped. "Why didn't *I* think of that?"

Every twinkle in her eyes returned. "So, who do we set up a room for? About now, almost every resident of little old Sweetgum is *already* in a happy relationship." She tapped her chin. "Should we find two singles?"

Benjamin chuckled. "Now, now… I wouldn't want to bother anyone. Plus, we'd have to compensate them for their time. And let's not forget that it might be *a little weird* to tell two strangers we've been watching them from afar."

Rochelle opened her mouth to speak, then paused. "You don't know these two kids, do you?"

"Nope."

"Alright, so who *does* test out the dream scheme?" She laughed. "Isn't that a catchy name?"

Benjamin's palms went cold. He tried to ignore the nervous rush filling his chest. "How about… *we* test it out ourselves?"

Rochelle blinked. "Huh?"

"If we experience our own test run, we'll know firsthand if it works." He smiled slyly. "After all, we're two single people."

Rochelle tapped her forehead lightly. "You know what? That *is* a great idea."

Benjamin exhaled, relieved. "Exactly. We're old, but we're *young at heart.*"

Rochelle arched a brow. "Old?"

Benjamin snickered. "We *are* old. But that's a blessing. And I have a feeling we'll attract couples of all ages."

Rochelle hesitated, then held out her fist. "Alright. Let's do it. Put 'er there, partner."

Benjamin could *sing.* He fist-bumped her and stood with open arms. "This sounds like a successful test run waiting to happen."

Rochelle hugged him. "Then you'll see—it's better to *trust* me than *doubt* me." She tapped his shoulder before heading for the door. "Now, if you'll excuse me, I got a diner to visit."

"Let me get the door for you."

Benjamin walked her across the soft carpet, trying not to beam too much at this remarkable new development.

CHAPTER ELEVEN

From the moment Rochelle stepped through the door, the comforting, buttery aroma of fresh espresso and roasted cocoa beans enveloped her senses. Roasted Beans Coffee Spot, with its high-arched windows and lively crowd, seemed to glow with a morning energy that put a little spring in her step. Garrulous customers chatted over steaming cups of lattes and cappuccinos, shaping the café into a picture-perfect spot—an uplifting portrait of Sweetgum's bustling Main Street. These days, every service establishment in town seemed to be booming, and Rochelle couldn't recall the last time she'd wandered into a place that didn't have a waitlist out the door. The success reminded her just how vibrant their community had become.

She clacked along the tiled floor in her wedge-heeled boots, relishing the freedom of not having any tables to serve herself. A long, impatient line twisted all the way back to the far corner, folks muttering gripes that were swallowed by the hum of the espresso machines. Rochelle tossed them a breezy wave.

"Don't worry, don't worry—no competition from me," she

said, her voice lilting across the café. "I'm not here to order anything."

She gave her flowing mauve coat a playful tug. She'd chosen it deliberately this chilly morning, the silky fabric fluttering around her knees with each brisk step. "And by right, places like this should have a VIP line for seniors anyway," she added, loud enough for a small group of older ladies in a corner booth to overhear.

A chorus of amused hums rose from the booth. One of the women, wearing a stylish knit cap, nodded. "Yes, ma'am, we sure do appreciate that idea," she called back.

Smiling, Rochelle made a little salute. Moments like these reminded her that she'd spent decades caring for people's appetites at her own diner—she understood the hectic morning rush all too well. The same tingle of adrenaline still whispered through her, recalling the days when she balanced multiple trays at once, fielded orders from left and right, and kept every single customer smiling. She might have stepped away from that life, but it lived on in her bones.

Finding a small gap by the counter, Rochelle leaned in and called, "Manager? Could I speak to your manager?" Her words soared above the hiss of steaming milk and the beep of timers. Despite the swirl of movement, the staff behind the counter looked dangerously close to meltdown.

A harried young barista whipped around, nearly spilling whipped cream from the silver canister he was holding. "Ma'am?" he yelped, steadying his hand at the last second. "A manager, you say? Um, yes, please—give me a second."

Rochelle chuckled, her eyes brimming with warmth. "Careful with that whipped cream, kiddo. We don't need you losing your job because of little old me."

His cheeks darkened with embarrassment as he capped the cup. "I'm so sorry. Didn't expect to hear someone yelling from the side there. But if you're Ms. Rochelle, come on back. Joanne's told me tons about you. Follow me through that door, ma'am."

Rochelle smoothed the lapel of her coat, privately enjoying the special treatment. "Thank you, son," she said. She slipped past the counter, exchanging polite nods with a few wide-eyed teens stationed at the espresso bar, then disappeared into the employees-only corridor.

~

A FEW MINUTES LATER, Rochelle found herself perched in a small, homey office that smelled of hazelnut coffee and fresh pastries. Two people faced her: Joanne, who was typing furiously on a laptop, and Xavier, who was flipping through a thick stack of papers. They both glanced up when she walked in, curiosity brightening their features.

"So, here's my idea," Rochelle began, crossing one leg elegantly over the other. "We're orchestrating a sweet little coffee date between two potential lovebirds, see? Old Benjy— uh, Mr. Walters—worried that local businesses might not be on board, but from the way you're looking at me, I'm guessing you're interested."

A vivid excitement sparkled in her eyes. Last night, she'd been up past midnight, drafting date-package concepts—fun experiences for couples who would stay at Benjamin's B&B. The brainstorming had her so wired that even her usual chamomile tea couldn't send her to sleep at a decent hour. She figured that feeling of being happily consumed by a project was exactly what her retirement had been missing.

"You could set up a special 'Lovebird Latte' or something along those lines for any couples who come in through Benjamin's place," Rochelle suggested, sweeping her arms in a showy gesture. "Bring them straight here for a cozy, coffee-themed date. What do you say?"

Joanne and Xavier exchanged quick, meaningful looks. Rochelle watched with anticipation as the pair communicated silently in that way married people sometimes do—finishing each other's thoughts without a word.

Finally, Joanne spun in her chair and broke into a grin. "Girl, I think this might be exactly what we need to push Roasted Beans from great to fantastic!" She high-fived Xavier, who was equally enthused.

"You hear that, Benjy?" Rochelle said under her breath, shoulders lifting with pride. "I knew they'd be game." She hopped out of her seat, retrieved her handbag from the floor, then gave the couple a bright smile. "Now, I'm heading to my next stop—Scoop There It Is. Gotta see how the ice cream parlor might fit into this plan."

"Wait, Rochelle!" Xavier leaned forward, his brow pinching. "Didn't you retire? How'd you get so involved with revamping a B&B?"

Joanne, who'd been typing just moments ago, now whirled around in her desk chair, beaming with curiosity. "Yes, do tell! Mr. Walters approached you? Oh, that's so adorable. And about that Christmas party last month—your gift exchange with him was practically the talk of the town. Everyone still mentions it!" She tugged at her sleek blazer, smoothing away invisible wrinkles. Rochelle marveled at how she and Xavier were both dressed sharply in matching suits, an obvious sign they'd been in important meetings all day.

"Mm-hmm," Xavier chimed in, adjusting his tie. "So, is it too bold to ask what he gave you? Because that whole scene was sweet enough to land in a holiday romance movie."

Rochelle took a quick breath, feeling her heart lurch at the memory of Benjamin's present. One minute, she'd been laughing with everyone at the diner, the next, she was holding a small, exquisitely wrapped box. "It was a lovely piece of jewelry." She kept her reply as level as she could, even though the recollection had her pulse fluttering. She still kept that necklace tucked away in a special spot. She hadn't worn it yet—perhaps because it felt too close to her heart, or perhaps because she hadn't worked out exactly what it symbolized.

Xavier and Joanne gushed a little, praising Benjamin's thoughtful nature.

Before they could fire off more questions and rope her into a full recap, Rochelle cleared her throat and took a step back toward the door. "Alright, you two, I'm off. Thanks for hopping on board. I'll be in touch soon." She beamed. "Mama's off to a good start!"

Making her exit, she sailed down the short hallway, confidence radiating from her. First meeting of the day down, and it had gone perfectly.

NEXT STOP: Scoop There It Is. Rochelle brisk-walked across two blocks of Main Street, her breath fogging in the cool air. She was determined to keep her momentum—no point letting her excitement die in the lull between meetings. As soon as she stepped into the cheery, pastel-colored shop, she spotted Rashad, the ice cream man, finishing up a milkshake for a customer.

"Rashad, hey!" Rochelle said, waving to grab his attention. The sugary scent of waffle cones and fudge swirled around her. Even on a chilly morning, the place hummed with visitors digging eagerly into cups and cones.

He handed off the milkshake with a flourish and swung around, the baby-blue towel on his shoulder swaying. "Ms. Rochelle, how's it going? What's up?"

"I have a proposition for you," she replied, leaning a forearm on the counter. "I need a special sundae or something romantic for couples visiting from the B&B. See, I'm putting it on the map as a perfect place for single folks, or couples in general, to get away and find love. And no love tour is complete without some sugary goodness to sweeten the deal."

Rashad let out a bright laugh, brushing a hand across his short beard. "You definitely came to the right man." He flexed an arm playfully, drawing attention to the wedding band glinting on his finger. "If there'd been a B&B in town that offered an all-out romance package years ago, I would've jumped on it before I tied the knot. That's a genius way to bring people together."

"People in Sweetgum sure do love to get hitched," Rochelle teased, nodding toward his ring. "How's your wife holding up? I bet you two are busy, especially with a baby on the way."

Rashad's eyes shone. "We're doing well, taking it one day at a time. India's at home resting up. She sends her love, by the way."

His mention of adding a new flavor or customizing the back booth for couples made Rochelle want to applaud. "See, that's the collaborative spark I'm talking about," she said. "I knew I picked the right place. Let's turn that little nook in the back into an ice-cream date paradise. String lights, maybe some rose petals. You pick. Romance up the wazoo."

Rashad waggled his brows. "I like the way you think. Let's do it."

Before Rochelle pivoted to leave, he stopped her. "When does this big plan officially launch? You calling all participating businesses to give them a heads-up, or should I brace for couples to start showing up and ordering triple sundaes at random?"

With a small grin, Rochelle mimicked holding a phone to her ear. "You'll get a call, dear. I promise." She thanked him again, breezed out the door, and took a few seconds on the sidewalk to catch her breath. "Whew. I am not as sprightly as I used to be," she murmured, pressing a hand to her chest. "Might be time to invest in a scooter."

Still, she felt almost giddy. Two out of three places had jumped on board without a single question or reservation. She smoothed her scarf, mentally mapping her approach for the final stop. People bustled around her on the sidewalk, the crisp air laced with the faint tang of salted pretzels from a nearby cart.

HER FINAL DESTINATION LOOMED AHEAD: a bright, stylish dance studio. The clerk at the front desk had directed her to the main practice room. Before Rochelle even fully opened the door, the brassy rhythm of salsa music spilled into the hallway, thrumming like a heartbeat in her ears. She stepped in, letting the bold, staccato notes soak into her bones.

"Ohh, yes," Rochelle breathed, swaying her hips in time. "Ooo-la-la indeed."

A line of women in neon workout gear pivoted gracefully under the direction of a tall, commanding instructor. His voice rose over the music, offering corrections and praise. Rochelle recognized him at once: Sean, Nevaeh's husband. She'd heard he was quite the dancer, but seeing him in action was a different story. He moved like someone half his age, exuding confidence with every step.

Over by the mirrored wall stood Nevaeh, phone in hand, filming the session. Rochelle broke into a wide grin and strutted in, giving her hips an exaggerated roll that sparked a round of laughs from the practicing women.

"Look at you, Ms. Rochelle!" one of them called. "You're a natural."

Rochelle chuckled as she glided over to Nevaeh and gently bumped her hip against the younger woman's in greeting.

"Oh gosh!" Nevaeh exclaimed, laughter bright in her eyes. She quickly tucked her phone away, then wrapped Rochelle in a warm hug. "If it isn't Ms. Newly Retired Diner Queen! How are you, ma'am?" She had to project her voice above the pulsing salsa.

Rochelle returned the hug with equal enthusiasm, catching a trace of floral body spray lingering on Nevaeh's sweater. "Doing great, sugar. But you know I like to stay busy. I'm here to talk to your hubby about a potential business collaboration. I'm about to take his dance studio—and hopefully a whole bunch of sweet couples—to the next level."

Nevaeh's eyes lit up with curiosity. "Oh? Tell me more," she said, but Rochelle just winked.

"All in due time, honey. Let me get his attention first."

Sean, catching sight of Rochelle, signaled for a short break in the session. The dancers trotted off to grab water bottles and towels, leaving the space to them.

"What's this I hear about taking my business to the next level?" he asked with a teasing lilt in his deep baritone. He used a remote to lower the music volume.

Rochelle introduced her plan: a dedicated dance lesson or class for visiting couples, integrated into Benjamin's newly minted romance packages. They could even host private sessions—two-person dance lessons that ended with a mini-performance under twinkling lights.

Nevaeh, eavesdropping from the side, gasped in delight. "That's so adorable, Ms. Rochelle! I can just imagine two shy lovebirds stepping onto the studio floor to learn salsa. How perfect."

Rochelle spread her hands in a flourish. "Right? A dash of excitement, a swirl of movement, hearts racing with every spin —that's some real bonding, if you ask me."

Sean listened intently, nodding every now and then. "I like the vision," he said, hooking his thumbs in the waistband of his workout pants. "You know I'm all about sharing the love, and this could bring new people into the studio, too. So count me in."

Those magic words were music to Rochelle's ears, nearly as good as the salsa playing in the background. "Well, that's all I needed to hear!" she declared, mind already buzzing with how she'd package this along with the other businesses. "We'll coordinate schedules, come up with a special couples' rate—maybe even a discount if they decide to attend a group class and socialize with other pairs. Thank you, Sean."

"Thank you, Ms. Rochelle," he replied warmly.

Triumph bubbled in her chest. She'd officially locked in all three businesses for the collaborative plan. As she exchanged a final hug with Nevaeh, she allowed herself a moment of pride. She'd set out to gather allies for Benjamin's bed-and-breakfast transformation, and every single one had said yes without hesitation.

The swirling salsa music kicked back up, and Rochelle offered the group a playful little wave. Then, with a big grin that nearly reached her ears, she spun on her heel and ducked out into the hallway.

"Oh, this is going to be so good," she whispered, picturing the faces of future guests—nervous single folks maybe, or established couples rediscovering their spark. Either way, she was convinced that what they were building was no ordinary getaway. And if the faint, excited flutter in her chest was anything to go by, Rochelle herself was a part of that magic, too.

Stepping outside, she found the cool air bracing, an instant reminder that she'd been dashing around town all morning. But it was a good kind of tired. She took in a deep breath, feeling the crisp air dance on her lips.

"Time to head home and give Benjy the good news," she murmured, glancing up at the winter sky. Then her lips quirked in a soft, private smile. "Maybe it's time to celebrate with something sweet myself."

And with that, she swept off down Main Street, her coat flapping behind her like a banner of triumph, confident that the sparks she'd ignited today would soon become the warm, glowing fire of new love stories in Sweetgum.

CHAPTER TWELVE

enjamin stood before the tall mirror in his bedroom, fiddling with the buttons of a red dress shirt that had somehow migrated to the back of his closet. He half wondered when he'd last worn this particular shirt; all he knew was that he liked the color on him. With a final tug at his cuffs, he exhaled, trying to quiet the flutter of nerves in his stomach.

"Get a grip, old man," he murmured, straightening his posture. "It's not like you haven't done this before."

But had he? It struck him that in all the time he'd been running the B&B alone, he'd never fussed over his clothing quite like this. He'd certainly never hovered by a mirror, checking if a shirt was too snug at the shoulders. Something about meeting Rochelle today—this test run, the so-called "date" that was definitely more than business—had him wanting everything to be just right.

Eventually, he tore himself away, stepping over scattered clothes he'd tried and rejected. Though a part of him whispered that Rochelle would probably tease him for caring so much, he couldn't help it. This was the same woman who'd brought new life into his B&B with her bold ideas. The same woman whose laugh he wanted to hear all afternoon, if he could manage it.

In the kitchen, he gulped down a quick piece of buttered toast. The aroma of coffee swirled around him, but he didn't bother pouring any. It made no sense to drink coffee at home when he was headed to Roasted Beans, where it would taste infinitely better—especially with Rochelle sitting across the table, swirling milk in her latte while she rattled off her latest plans.

Outside, the early-winter sun glinted on fresh patches of snow. Benjamin zipped up his coat and braced himself for the chill as he locked the B&B's front door. He paused to glance around the property, admiring the evergreens dusted white, thinking how pretty the greenhouse looked in winter. Then, drawing a calming breath, he set off toward Main Street.

BY THE TIME Benjamin arrived at Roasted Beans Coffee Spot, the shop was in full swing: baristas flew between espresso machines, milk steamers hissed and gurgled, and a lively crowd filled every table. Hints of vanilla, cinnamon, and roasted coffee hung in the air. The space exuded a cozy chaos he found endearing.

He spotted Rochelle instantly. She was seated at a corner table, chatting with Joanne—one of the owners. Rochelle wore a dusky-purple sweater and a patterned scarf that caught the light in subtle flashes. Her posture was relaxed, though her eyes scanned the shop with that familiar can-do energy he'd come to admire. She turned, caught sight of him, and offered a brief, warm smile.

"Mr. Benjamin," she said, lifting her hand in a casual wave. "You made it."

Benjamin tugged off his gloves and stepped closer, his heart giving the slightest jump at how happy she looked to see him. "Wouldn't miss it," he said. He nodded at Joanne, who was beaming from ear to ear.

"Well, look at you two," Joanne teased, sliding a tray onto the table. "I've got something special this morning—house-made vanilla latte with just a dash of cinnamon. Thought you might like it."

Rochelle's smile widened when she spotted the foam art: the steamers had shaped a swirl of milk into two neat initials—B and R. "That's adorable," she said with an amused shake of her head, glancing at Benjamin. "Joanne's always fancying up people's drinks."

Benjamin took a seat and settled his coat on the back of the chair. "You know," he told Joanne, "I might be back here more often if you keep spoiling us like this."

"Then it's a deal," Joanne quipped, shooting him a wink before disappearing behind the busy counter.

Benjamin turned to Rochelle, letting his gaze linger for a moment. "You look nice," he said, voice gentler than he intended.

Her cheeks warmed slightly—he saw it in the subtle shift of her expression—and she lowered her eyes to the latte. "Not too shabby yourself." She clinked her cup lightly against his. "So. Ready to do this?"

He gave her a playful half-smile. "Should I be worried?"

"Depends," she replied, sipping her latte. Her lips curved around the rim, and she let out a pleased hum at the taste. "If you can handle a thorough test of my grand matchmaking ideas, you'll be just fine."

Benjamin leaned in, bracing his forearms on the table. "So how does this 'test run' work, exactly?" He tried not to grin too widely, but there was no helping the bubble of anticipation in his chest.

Rochelle's eyes danced. "Remember, this was your idea. A

live rehearsal of sorts—seeing if we can plan a day of shared activities that fosters closeness. Then, if it works out for us, it'll work for future singles or couples at the B&B." She shrugged, the movement sending a gentle ripple through her scarf. "At least, that's the theory."

Benjamin nodded. "So… we're basically going on a date," he teased, pausing to blow on his latte.

She raised a brow, gaze flicking away. "Let's call it a test date." Beneath her playful tone, Benjamin sensed the faintest undercurrent of nerves. He found it oddly reassuring—he wasn't the only one feeling the weight of this.

He took a careful sip of coffee, savoring the sweetness of the vanilla, and let the smooth warmth settle in his chest. "Alright, Ms. Rochelle. Test date it is. Lead the way."

Rochelle checked the time on her phone. "First stop is visiting that new dessert place on Fifth—Jovon's. You know he's an incredible pastry chef. I arranged for us to sample some 'couples' creations he's been perfecting." She lifted a small notepad from her purse, flipping through it. "Then, we'll swing by the dance studio—I might have convinced the owner to give us a mini-lesson."

Benjamin swallowed, picturing himself attempting dance steps in front of Rochelle. "A dance lesson, huh? You're trying to show me up?"

"I'd never do such a thing," she answered, eyes twinkling. "But for our guests, a dance class could be a fun bonding experience." She tapped her pen on the pad. "If we manage not to trip over each other's feet, we'll have proof it can work."

His response was lost in a laugh. "I can handle a little two-step," he claimed with more confidence than he felt.

Rochelle shot him a knowing look. "We'll see about that."

A comfortable quiet settled between them as they finished their lattes. Benjamin watched Rochelle's gaze roam the café— she greeted a few patrons with friendly waves, nodded at Joanne when she passed by, and made small talk with a barista about new flavors. Something about the way she moved through a room—like she was always half hostess, half guest—spoke to her history running the diner. It was second nature for her to make spaces feel like home.

When they'd drained the last of their coffee, Rochelle collected her notes. "We should get going," she said. "Jovon hates it when people are late. He'll tease us mercilessly if we show up behind schedule."

Benjamin stood, helping her into her coat. "Wouldn't want that," he joked, though his heart gave another jump at the simple act of draping her coat around her shoulders.

She paused, glancing up at him as she slid her arms through the sleeves. The moment stretched, charged with an anticipation that made his pulse quicken. Then she cleared her throat, offering a small, private smile. "C'mon, Romeo," she teased, heading for the door. "Time to see if this test date idea actually holds water."

OUTSIDE, a breeze carried the scent of roasted chestnuts from a nearby vendor. The sidewalks gleamed with a thin coating of slush, and overhead, the sky was a bright winter blue. Benjamin inhaled deeply, stepping beside Rochelle as they navigated the crowded street.

"How's business at the B&B?" she asked over the hum of passing cars.

"Not bad," he replied, tucking his hands into his pockets to keep them warm. "Bookings are steady, but I'd love to see them climb. If this romance angle pans out, I'll have to hire extra staff."

"Hire them," Rochelle said confidently. "You'll need them."

He chuckled. "You sound so sure."

She lifted a shoulder in a half-shrug. "When you've run a business for decades, you pick up a feel for what'll click."

Their footsteps kept pace with each other, an effortless stride that made it feel as though they'd been walking side by side for years. Soon, Jovone's dessert shop came into view—its front window festooned with pink and white balloons, a sign reading *Sweet Indulgences* shining in cursive letters.

"You ready?" Rochelle asked, pausing at the door.

Benjamin gave her a mock salute. "Lead on, Ms. Rochelle."

She pushed the door open, and a wave of sugary warmth spilled over them—vanilla, chocolate, caramel, all melding into one tempting swirl. They found Jovone behind the counter, plating slices of cake so elaborate, they could've been sculptures.

Jovone grinned when he saw them. "Ah, my favorite duo!" he proclaimed, wiping his hands on a towel. "Right on time, too. Follow me—I've set up something special in the back."

Benjamin shared a quick look with Rochelle, who shot him a smile that made his stomach flip. *This is actually fun,* he thought, letting Jovone lead them toward a small side table laden with pastries, sample spoons, and a pile of napkins.

"Feast your eyes," Jovone declared, gesturing grandly.

They surveyed the mini feast: a "lovers' sundae" topped with fresh berries, two forks for a decadent chocolate slice labeled "Kiss of Midnight," and tiny heart-shaped pastries dusted with sugar. Rochelle let out an appreciative hum. "You're outdoing yourself, Jovone."

"Just wait till you taste it," the chef teased. "But first—" He lifted his phone. "I need a picture to post on social media. If folks see you two enjoying this stuff, they'll be clamoring for it by the weekend."

Benjamin and Rochelle exchanged amused looks. "Go for it," Benjamin said, trying not to laugh at how official Jovone suddenly appeared, phone poised for the perfect shot.

"You might have to, y'know, get a little closer," Jovone hinted with a mischievous wink.

Rochelle lifted her chin, feigning nonchalance. But she stepped closer to Benjamin, and in response, he placed one hand gently at the small of her back. She tensed briefly, then relaxed against him. A soft flush colored her cheeks, and Benjamin's heart gave a sudden leap. When was the last time he'd been this close to her outside of the B&B?

As Jovone snapped a few pictures, Rochelle reached for a sample spoon. "Alright, enough paparazzi. I'm starving."

In short order, they were giggling through the over-the-top sundae, passing forks back and forth and letting each other have the best bite of chocolate cake. The playful banter and shared sips of melted ice cream felt...intimate. Rochelle's hand brushed his more than once, sending a pleasant buzz up his arm. Every time, she'd cast him a fleeting, half-embarrassed grin that said, *Let's ignore that but also maybe not ignore it.*

Eventually, Jovone backed off, giving them space to taste and take notes. Rochelle scribbled on her notepad, leaning over to show Benjamin her bullet points: *Dessert portion too big? Maybe smaller, plus add flavor combos?*

"You really are analyzing every detail," Benjamin murmured in awe.

She shrugged. "That's the point, right?"

She took one more bite of cake, humming contentedly. Then, without warning, she lifted a spoonful of whipped cream toward Benjamin. "Here. Try a bit with the raspberry sauce."

He obliged, opening his mouth—only to have Rochelle laugh and jerk the spoon away at the last second, leaving him to sputter in surprise.

Jovone cackled from across the room, calling out, "Get her back, man!"

Benjamin just shook his head, a grin sneaking onto his face. He snagged a spare spoon, scooped up a bit of cream, and flicked it at Rochelle. She dodged, letting out a squeak. A few pink droplets landed on her sweater, and she snorted in mock outrage.

"All right, you two," Jovone scolded between laughs. "Don't ruin my fancy sweets. Some of us have to run a respectable business here."

Rochelle wiped her sleeve, still chuckling, and Benjamin found himself thinking that if this day was supposed to be a rehearsal for potential couples, it was doing a number on his own heart. He couldn't recall the last time something as simple as sharing dessert had left him feeling so alive.

"Alright," Rochelle said at last, tapping the back of her pen against the notepad. "We've got what we need. Jovone, you're a genius. We'll recommend you as the place to come for 'dessert for two.'"

The pastry chef gave them an exaggerated bow. "Music to my ears."

Benjamin thanked him, then put a hand gently on Rochelle's elbow, guiding her back toward the front of the shop. The hustle and bustle of Sweet Indulgences seemed to swirl around them in a sugary haze.

Outside, the breeze was sharper than before, and they both shivered as they stepped onto the sidewalk. Rochelle checked her watch, biting her lip with a faint grin. "We're running a little behind schedule, so we'd better hustle if we want to make that dance lesson."

"Lead on," Benjamin said, tucking his hands into his pockets. "I'm all yours."

For a heartbeat, Rochelle's eyes flickered with something soft, something almost vulnerable. Then she turned away, calling over her shoulder, "Don't complain if I step on your toes!"

Benjamin followed with a chuckle. "If I do, I'll take it up with the manager."

She huffed a laugh, and together, they set off toward the dance studio, the winter sun spotlighting their path.

All the while, Benjamin's mind whirled with the realization that, for a so-called "test run," this was feeling a whole lot like a real date. And part of him hoped it might turn into something more than just a marketing gimmick. If Rochelle sensed it, she gave no sign—at least not yet. But from the playful gleam in her eyes, he wondered if maybe she felt the same warmth in the pit of her stomach that he did.

Either way, as they walked side by side, hot chocolate swirling in his stomach and the memory of her laughter still ringing in his ears, Benjamin decided there was nowhere else he'd rather be.

CHAPTER THIRTEEN

Rochelle speared a crispy chicken tender with her fork, savoring the sizzling crunch that echoed through Malachi's cozy apartment. She could smell the warm spice mix—paprika, a touch of garlic—rising from the steaming plate. As she cut into the tender, she marveled at how far Malachi's space had come.

"It's like you two are working backward," she teased, popping the bite into her mouth. The flavorful burst of pepper and salt danced on her tongue, forcing her to pause before continuing. She swallowed, dabbed her lips with a napkin, and gestured with her fork toward her nephew. "Start a business together first, then date, get engaged, and now you're thinking about moving in together?"

Across the small dinner table, Malachi and Aimee exchanged that knowing look couples used when they understood each other without words. Rochelle's curiosity spiked—she recognized that particular brand of intimacy from seeing countless couples fall in love at her diner back in the day.

"That's exactly why we work," Aimee said, grinning as she spooned baked beans over her mashed potatoes. The swirl of savory brown beans mixing with buttery potatoes made Rochelle's stomach growl with approval. "It makes us special."

Rochelle exhaled a soft laugh, her gaze sweeping the once-sparse apartment. She remembered when Malachi first moved in—plain white walls, a lumpy couch, a TV precariously propped on a makeshift stand. Now, life had fully taken root here. The comforting aroma of home-cooked food mingled with a gentle vanilla candle flickering on the kitchen counter. A red dish towel hung neatly over the oven handle, and an inviting fruit basket, brimming with apples and bananas, brightened the modest table. Even a pair of fuzzy socks—most definitely not Malachi's—peeked out from under the coffee table.

It's amazing what love can do to a place, Rochelle thought, her heart warming. She had a sneaking suspicion Aimee's touch was behind every bit of color and coziness.

Malachi, who'd been inhaling his meal like a man starved all day, finally slowed down enough to catch a breath. "That's right," he said, using the back of his hand to wipe his mouth. "So, what do you think about us moving into a bungalow in the new housing complex? We've looked at a few places, but nothing feels quite right yet."

Rochelle took another chicken tender, cutting off a bite-sized piece before responding. "Don't stress yourselves out. You'll know the right place when you find it. Trust me." She recalled her own transitions—purchasing her first home, then letting it go when she retired. Houses weren't just structures; they held memories, even the future ones you hadn't made yet.

Aimee and Malachi launched into talk of how the diner was bustling. Their enthusiastic chatter wove through tales of new menu items, unexpected crowds, and Malachi's growing reputation as a local hero of sorts. Rochelle felt a glow of pride settle in her chest. Whenever people spoke about her nephew, they did so with genuine warmth—something Malachi himself seemed oblivious to.

"Well, folks in this town like to see new faces taking on old traditions," Rochelle said, finishing the last bite of her chicken tender. She pointed her fork at Malachi. "And you, my dear nephew, have no idea how important you've become around here."

Malachi snorted. "Oh, hush. You're exaggerating."

"I'm not," Rochelle insisted, lips curving into a smile. "I hear it every time I go out for groceries. 'Malachi's done this, Malachi's done that...' They adore you."

He ducked his head, ears tinged with embarrassment. Aimee shot him a fond grin, patting his arm.

Then, with the timing of a comedian, Malachi leaned back in his chair and smirked. "Oh, by the way..." He took a deliberate sip from his glass of lemonade—drawing it out just to build suspense. "A little birdie told me businesses on Main Street are about to see an even bigger boom. Something about a certain project brewing?"

Aimee mirrored his conspiratorial expression, tapping her chin. "Mhmm. And from what I hear, it sounds a lot like that hypothetical hotel idea you wanted my help typing up last week, Rochelle." She waggled her brows, her brown eyes gleaming with playful mischief. "Ring a bell?"

Rochelle exhaled sharply, the sound almost a sigh. She set her juice glass down with a soft clink that betrayed her mild annoyance. "Ah, nuts. Word's already spreading?"

Malachi and Aimee burst out laughing, their combined joy filling the small apartment. Rochelle tried to maintain a calm face, but a hint of a grin tugged at her lips. *It's impossible to stay grumpy around these two,* she thought, though she'd never say it out loud.

"Relax, Aunt Rochelle," Malachi said, lifting his palms in mock-surrender. "No one's saying it's a bad idea." He cut a quick glance at Aimee, eyes sparkling. "We just find it hilarious how you tried to keep it under wraps for so long."

Aimee nodded eagerly. "Your plans for the B&B sound genius! Turning it into a singles retreat where people can meet in person instead of swiping on their phones? That's a brilliant concept."

Rochelle allowed her shoulders to sink, tension easing as she let out a self-satisfied smile. "Right? I'm feeling pretty confident about it now. At first, I worried it'd be a flop, but it's really starting to come together." She lifted her juice again, taking a sip before setting it down. "All Benjamin wanted was a slight boost in occupancy, but I'm telling you"—she waved her hand, as though painting a grand picture—"we're taking it to another level."

A new thought tickled the back of her mind. *What would Malachi, with his savvy, have to say about this?* She turned toward him, chewing on her bottom lip thoughtfully. "Actually, since you've got more business sense than half the people I know, what do you think? I didn't want you two finding out before I had all the details, but—"

"Why not?" Aimee interrupted, her usually cheerful tone dipping slightly. She placed a hand on her chest, eyes earnest. "Did you think we'd judge you? Rochelle, you know I'm one of your number one supporters. Whatever you decide, I'll back you up."

Malachi, mouth full of mashed potatoes, hurriedly swallowed so he could speak. "I think Aunt Rochelle worried we'd tell her to rest," he said, tossing Aimee a knowing look. "We have been on her case about slowing down for ages, huh?"

Rochelle tried to roll her eyes, but couldn't deny the truth. They had certainly reminded her often enough to "take it easy." Aimee giggled, nodding.

"Sure," Malachi went on, "but we also knew you'd find your way into another project sooner or later. Retirement rarely sticks for someone as active as you." He paused, his voice softening. "You know, the folks who give up all their hobbies after retiring... Sometimes they waste away."

Rochelle bobbed her head in agreement. "Oh yeah. Remember Mrs. Smith?"

Aimee's face scrunched, then recognition lit her features. "Oh, Mrs. Smith!" She let out a small sigh, shoulders slumping. "She's in a home now, isn't she? She never really did anything after retiring."

Rochelle nodded, feeling a slight ache in her heart. "Didn't move around much, stopped socializing... She lost her mobility. Now she's barely able to get out and about." For a moment, the three of them sat in mutual empathy, the only sound the wind rattling the windows.

A hush settled. Rochelle found herself looking around Malachi's apartment again—at the little signs of life and progress—and let her thoughts wander. *I won't let myself fade like that,* she resolved, aware that the diner had been her lifeblood for decades. Now, with the B&B, she had a fresh sense of purpose.

Shaking off the somber note, she squared her shoulders. "Alright, let's not get morose," she said, clearing her throat. "Mal, you're ten steps ahead of everyone else, so I have to ask: What's our next big move with the B&B?"

Malachi set aside his plate and grabbed his laptop, perched on the counter. "Easy," he declared. "You need to revamp the website. The concept is genius, but if your online presence doesn't match, you'll lose interest before guests even step foot in the door."

Rochelle blinked. "Huh. Why didn't I think of that?"

"That's why I'm here," Malachi replied, grinning. He opened his laptop, tapping a few keys before spinning the screen to face Rochelle. "See this? The layout is outdated, and the photo quality is all over the place. You want something sleek, modern, easy to navigate—people judge a business's vibe in under a minute online."

Aimee sprang into action like a co-conspirator, collecting empty plates and ferrying them to the sink. "Let's do it," she said, tying up her long hair with a scrunchie. "We'll help you right now."

Rochelle felt an unexpected surge of gratitude. *Here they are, dropping everything to help me,* she thought, a tingle of appreciation warming her chest. Malachi quickly tossed out suggestions for new color themes and fonts while Aimee rinsed dishes, occasionally chiming in with marketing tips from her own experiences.

The sounds of running water, clinking dishes, and the occasional beep of Malachi's laptop keys filled the cozy apartment. Rochelle jotted notes on a spare napkin, nodding along to their ideas. Sleek, modern, easy to navigate, she repeated mentally, scribbling down star icons next to the must-haves.

Eventually, they wrapped up, with Malachi's rough mock-up of a new homepage displayed on the screen and Aimee's scribbled bullet points pinned down in Rochelle's notepad. Rochelle sat back, running a hand through her hair. "I was a fool to keep you two out of this," she admitted. "Look at how much we got done in one evening."

Aimee beamed, her cheeks slightly flushed from the warm steam in the kitchen. "That's what we're here for."

A satisfied quiet settled over them—until Aimee's eyes sparkled with renewed mischief. "Sooo..." She drew out the word, sliding into the chair across from Rochelle. "What's going on with you and Benjamin?"

The question struck Rochelle like a stray gust of cold air. She kept her features neutral, though her pulse gave a tiny jump. "What do you mean, 'what's going on'? We're working together to take his business to the next level."

Malachi snorted. "Aunt Rochelle, c'mon, you can't fool us."

Rochelle's cheeks heated under their combined scrutiny. "I'm not 'fooling' anyone," she insisted, though she wasn't fully convinced herself. The memory of Benjamin's steady gaze and warm laugh surfaced unbidden in her mind—along with the lingering echoes of their recent "test run" date.

Aimee leaned forward, lips curving in a conspiratorial grin. "You sure there's nothing else? I mean, you're basically the town's top matchmaker—and you've got all these ideas about finding love for others." She paused dramatically, letting the implication sink in. "Let's just say, I'd be surprised if none of it rubbed off on you."

Rochelle set her jaw, wishing her flush would vanish. "Listen, I am a grown woman who has accepted that love isn't in the cards for me." The words emerged with practiced finality.

Silence stretched between them, broken only by the hum of the refrigerator. But in that stillness, Rochelle felt the faint tremor in her own resolve. She'd said those words for so long—*love isn't for me*—that repeating them had become second nature. Yet now, a tiny voice inside whispered a quiet, pointed question: *Are you absolutely sure?*

She didn't have an answer. And for the first time in a long while, she found that uncertainty… strangely exhilarating.

CHAPTER FOURTEEN

Who would have thought that a little corner at the back of an ice cream parlor could turn into such a spectacle?

The soft hum of a jazz melody drifted through the shop, mingling with the sugary scent of waffle cones and melting chocolate. Behind the counter, Rashad—proud owner of *Scoop There It Is*—grinned as he gestured toward the bright pink table at the heart of his latest innovation.

"You can mix flavors, pile on as many toppings as you want —get creative with it," he explained, rubbing his hands together in satisfaction. Small glass bowls, arranged in a neat rainbow of color, sat in the middle of the table. And at its center, the star of the show—a glistening, untouched sundae, waiting to be transformed.

Benjamin let out a low whistle, placing his hands on his hips. "Well, I'll be. This is something else."

Outside, the sky was a brilliant, wintry blue, the kind that only showed itself on the tail end of winter. A few snowflakes fluttered lazily to the ground, one or two catching in Benjamin's hair as he and Rochelle had walked over from the diner. There weren't many customers in the shop, which gave Rashad ample time to guide them through the process.

"So, we just decorate our snack however we want?" Benjamin turned to Rochelle with a grin.

She smiled back, but it didn't quite reach her eyes.

Since he'd picked her up, she'd been quieter than usual, her usual spark dampened like a flame behind a fogged-up window.

Rashad, sensing none of this, rested his hands on his hips. "Pretty much, Mr. Walters. I figured letting folks build their own sundae would be a fun way for them to get to know each other. That's how it worked for me and India, after all." He dusted an invisible speck from his pristine pink sleeve.

Rochelle pulled her hands close to her lips, nodding in approval. "It sure did. And this looks incredible, Rashad. I think it'll be a hit." She patted his back lightly before ushering him back to the counter. "Alright, Benjy. Let's test this out before our dance lesson." She glanced at her watch before quickly sitting down. "And before our sundaes melt."

Benjamin chuckled, settling in across from her. "That sure is right." He rubbed his hands together as he surveyed the assortment of toppings. Gummy bears, chocolate chips, sour worms, almonds—so many options, each one tempting in its own way. "Back in my day, all we had was syrup," he remarked, watching Rochelle pick up a bowl of almonds. "We're going with almonds?"

She held the bowl aloft, one brow raised. "That depends. Do you *want* almonds, Mr. Walters? We both have to eat this, so we should be on the same page."

Benjamin's gaze flickered to her face, noticing again the small dimness in her eyes, the way her smile didn't stretch to its full brilliance. Something was weighing on her. But instead of pressing, he decided to play along.

"I like almonds," he assured her. "Go ahead, Miss."

Satisfied, Rochelle sprinkled the salted almonds over the ice cream. "Alright, now you pick something."

Benjamin rubbed the back of his neck. "There's just so much." He laughed, eying the gummy bears before shifting toward the pretzels sitting near her side of the table. "Everything looks either *too* sweet or *too* salty."

"How often do you eat sweets?" Rochelle asked, already reaching for the pretzels as if she'd read his mind.

Benjamin smiled, shaking his head. "Not often. I try to keep desserts to a minimum. I know I'm close to the grave, but I'm not sprinting toward it."

That got a real smile out of her—just for a second. "That's exactly why you should *go crazy* with food every now and then," she said, tossing four pretzels into the mix. A flicker of amusement danced across her face. "Especially for folks like us whose graves practically follow them."

Her voice was lighter now, edged with her usual playfulness, but Benjamin could tell she was forcing it. Still, he played along, hoping to keep that brightness going.

"When it comes to old heads," Rochelle continued, "the saying *we're here for a good time, not a long time* rings truer than ever."

Then, without warning, she grabbed the gummy bears and dumped the entire bowl onto the sundae.

Benjamin blinked. "Uh—was that intentional?"

Rochelle popped one into her mouth, chewing thoughtfully. "Mmhmm." Then, grinning mischievously, she stretched across the table and placed one against his lips.

Without thinking, Benjamin stuck out his tongue, letting her place the candy there. As he chewed, the bright, sour burst of flavor hit his tongue, and something unexpected bubbled up in his chest.

Laughter.

The sheer ridiculousness of it—being hand-fed like a child,

sharing a bowl of ice cream like a couple of teenagers—was enough to make him chuckle. Rochelle's laughter followed, light and free.

"It's refreshing, isn't it?" she teased.

"It is," Benjamin admitted. He scooped up another handful, tossing them into his mouth. "Feels like sneaking candy before dinner."

"My mother would've sent me to my room if I tried that," Rochelle mused, now nibbling on chocolate chips.

Benjamin held out his palm, requesting some. She placed a few in his hand, and they both chewed in contentment, the world around them momentarily shrinking down to this ridiculous little sundae and the shared moment between them.

"You know what?" Rochelle picked up a bowl of peanut sticks and unceremoniously dumped them into the sundae. "We should just throw *everything* on top."

Benjamin grinned. "Now *that's* the spirit." He grabbed the strawberry syrup and squeezed a generous amount over the mountain of toppings. The once-pristine sundae was now an explosion of colors and textures—a mess of flavors that made absolutely no sense together. And yet, somehow, it was perfect.

"We are *insane*," Rochelle declared, laughing as she added a final shower of sprinkles.

Benjamin leaned back, watching her with a quiet sort of admiration. She was back to her wild, prideful self—the Rochelle he adored in every form. But even in moments like these, he'd take any version of her that came his way.

Five minutes later, Rashad returned, eyeing their creation with open-mouthed amusement. "Alright, I gave y'all enough time to create something epic. Let's see what we're working with."

He leaned over the table, hands on his hips, brow furrowing as he took in the *masterpiece.* "Wow."

Rochelle tossed her silk scarf over her shoulder, crossing one leg over the other smugly. "This, my dear Rashad, is the *B&B Special*—ready to be placed *immediately* on your menu."

Benjamin, feeding off her energy, lifted his spoon. "And I'm sure it tastes *incredible.*"

He took a large bite.

Then froze.

Good *Lord.*

Rashad doubled over in laughter. "Your face says everything."

Rochelle, meanwhile, struck a playful pose. "Pose for the camera, Benjy."

Benjamin tried to smile, but between the overwhelming sugar rush and the flash of Rashad's camera, all he could focus on was Rochelle's expression—radiant, mischievous, completely *in her element.*

And somehow, he couldn't look away.

THE SIDEWALK WAS MOSTLY empty as they walked to the dance studio, the late afternoon sun casting long golden streaks across the pavement.

Benjamin basked in the warmth of it, hands tucked into his coat pockets. "So, what do you think the chances are that Rashad actually puts our sundae on the menu?"

Rochelle scoffed. "If he doesn't, he'll definitely *steal* our idea." She gripped the strap of her bag as they walked. "That was fun."

"It really was," Benjamin agreed.

For a long moment, they simply walked in step, listening to the rhythm of their own footfalls.

Then, softly—so softly that he almost missed it—Rochelle said, "I hope I didn't scare you back there."

Benjamin frowned. "Scare me?"

"With all my talk about us being *close to the grave.*"

Benjamin scratched his arm. "What? Of course not. You were right." He exhaled, glancing at her. "We only have so much time left. It's harder for those we leave behind."

And as Rochelle sighed, arms folding tight against the cold, Benjamin knew—there was more to her silence today than just a simple off-mood.

She had a past.

And it was time to finally hear it.

CHAPTER FIFTEEN

That had gone even better than she thought it would.

Rochelle couldn't stop smiling. The glow on her face had lingered since the moment she'd said goodbye to Benjamin last Friday after their test date. Now it was Monday evening, and flashes of the day still popped into her head—his carefree laugh, the reassuring warmth in his eyes, even the subtle way his fingertips brushed her waist when they danced. Every detail played in her mind like a highlight reel.

Her apartment mirror had practically teased her all weekend: each time she caught her own reflection, she'd notice that same giddy expression, as if she were a teenager fresh from a first date. Rochelle had no intention of admitting that to anyone, of course, but there was no denying the excitement fluttering inside her.

Admitting the truth about Brian had been terrifying, but after hearing Benjamin's gentle response, she was so glad she had. Only Mei knew how that relationship had unraveled—and how it left Rochelle doubting her own worth. Now, someone else carried that piece of her story. Strangely, that made it feel less like a burden and more like a step toward healing.

She hummed softly to herself as she carried a tray of golden-brown pizza pockets out of the oven. Heat radiated from the tray, and the savory scent of baked cheese, tangy tomato, and flaky pastry crust wafted upward, promising comfort and satisfaction. It was the kind of smell that invited conversation, and even better company.

In the back of the diner, murmuring voices and muffled giggles floated through the partially closed door. Rochelle's brow lifted in mild curiosity.

Tonight was book club night, and she'd taken the liberty of preparing their snack. Over the weekend, she'd forced herself to catch up on their latest read—despite sweet memories of dancing and laughing with Benjamin, rushing in whenever her mind wandered from the page. Still, she wasn't sure how focused she'd be tonight. That man had a hold on her—she'd almost confessed something else to him, something she wasn't even ready to admit to herself yet.

As she pushed through the kitchen doors and made her way to the counter, she noticed the murmuring die down. Several of the women—including Mei with her silver-bell earrings tinkling—regarded her with looks that were just a little too pleased.

Suspicious.

"Alright, here it is, ladies. Nice and hot." She set the silver tray in the middle of the table, meeting their collective gaze with a faint frown. "Sorry for the gals watching their figures, but we're having pizza pockets this evening."

A satisfied chorus of "oohs" and "ahhs" rippled through the group as hands eagerly reached for the food. Rochelle took a seat at the curved booth beside Mei, brushing stray crumbs from her apron.

Mrs. Bridges snapped her fingers happily. "These look good, Roche. Can't remember the last time I had something cheesy."

Rochelle slid her hand over the tabletop, checking for any

stray flour. "Well, you're welcome. Doctor says variety is essential in old age. Means with food, too."

She scanned the faces around the table. Nevaeh beamed like the cat that got the cream, and Brandi wore a knowing smirk. A hush settled, charged with hushed excitement.

Rochelle's stomach dipped—she knew that look. It was the look of a group with news they were dying to share.

Finally, she narrowed her eyes. "What's going on with you all?" she demanded, crossing her arms. "You're smiling like a bunch of teens on prom night."

One thing about Rochelle? She hated secrets—especially when they concerned her. She prided herself on staying in the know, not being the one left out of it.

Mei slapped the table, her eyes dancing with mischief. "I may have filled them in on everything going on with you and Benjamin."

Rochelle's heart jolted. And just like that, the floodgates burst open.

"Sean said you two got really close on your dance lesson date. Did you kiss?" Nevaeh blurted, words tumbling out so fast Rochelle could barely track them. "Mrs. Zhang swore she saw you!"

Rochelle's eyes popped wide. "She said what?" She rounded on Mei, her voice tight with disbelief.

"Somebody caught you two holding up traffic on the sidewalk," Mrs. Craskin added, chewing noisily on a pizza pocket. "Said you were staring at the clouds together last Friday."

Rochelle blinked. "Staring at the clouds? Now who told you that?"

"I was hoping your test date would bring you to the coffee shop so I could witness the chemistry," Joanne piped in, practically vibrating with excitement. "Nevaeh's sister told her that her husband saw you two laughing and holding hands over your special sundae!" She clapped her hands. "I heard you even named it after your couple name!"

Rochelle sputtered. "Our... 'couple name'? Where on earth—?"

"People saw you holding hands!" Courtney declared, forming a heart shape with her fingers. She gave Rochelle a pointed grin.

"I heard you blocked traffic because folks were too distracted by you two being all lovey-dovey near the ice cream parlor," Brandi chimed.

"And I heard you're so in love, you can't be bothered to get to the diner at your usual time," Mrs. Bridges said in a theatrical hush, waving two pizza pockets like gavels. "Now, why haven't you shared any of this with us, Rochelle?"

Their voices merged into one chaotic swirl, each rumor more outrageous than the last. Rochelle's mind reeled. Gossip never died in this town—it multiplied like rabbits, and apparently she was the main attraction this week.

"HEY!" she suddenly shouted.

Silence fell. Every eye locked on her.

Rochelle grabbed Mei's arm, pointing over her head. "Whatever this woman tells you is made up. She's been fantasizing about me and that man for months." She turned a glare on the others. "We are strictly business, okay? Don't take anything Mei says as gospel—and don't believe every piece of gossip floating around this town."

To emphasize, she dropped her handbag onto the table with a thud. "Now, let's talk Chapter Five of *Love-Sick Paradise*."

Inwardly, Rochelle winced, realizing too late what a romance novel discussion would invite.

Predictably, the story was romantic—very romantic.

They opened their books, flipping pages to the assigned chapter. Yet the new hush had a tense undercurrent, as though the group was just waiting for an excuse to pounce again.

Mrs. Bridges struck first, her voice brimming with glee. "My favorite part was when that big, strong, handsome hero rescued our main girl from the flowing river of desire," she declared, arching her brows in Rochelle's direction. "Even though she pretended she didn't like being in his arms, we all know she did."

A wicked gleam lit the older woman's eyes. "Maybe one day she'll drop the denial, too."

Laughter erupted around them, echoing in the diner's stillness.

Rochelle rolled her eyes, but her lips twitched. They had her pegged, and they knew it. "That's your take, huh? Fine. I can admit the heroine's protests seemed half-hearted." She shrugged. "But—" raising a single finger, "not every situation is the same."

"Uh-huh," Brandi sing-songed, tapping the side of her book.

Nevaeh shot up a hand. "Can I just say what I think?"

Rochelle sighed. "Go on, then."

Nevaeh's grin nearly split her face. "I think you should take Mr. Walters on a *real* date. None of this 'test date' business. Something that's just for the two of you."

Joanne immediately nodded. "Oh, I second that idea, wholeheartedly! Then you can stop hiding behind business as an excuse, Rochelle."

Brandi chuckled. "You'll never know for sure unless you explore."

Rochelle felt heat crawling up her neck. The group pressed in, figuratively at least, their gazes urging her to spill something personal, to confirm the rumors swirling in Sweetgum.

She hastily flipped back to *Love-Sick Paradise*, focusing on the swirling font on page one-hundred. "The character in our book goes on crazy adventures in Chapter Five," she remarked, skimming lines to anchor the conversation. "Just like you did with Benjamin last week!" Mei said, practically bouncing in her seat. Her silver-bell earrings jingled like tiny conspirators.

"Oh, for heaven's sake—" Rochelle growled, reaching over to tug Mei's dangling earring in mock punishment. "We're not talking about me anymore."

Across the table, Courtney grinned. "Challenge: Rochelle stops denying she likes Mr. Walters." She mimed dropping a microphone.

Laughter reverberated again, spiking Rochelle's frustration mixed with a reluctant amusement. She tossed her book aside. "Fine!" Her voice was louder than intended, but she was beyond caring. She linked her fingers tightly on the table. "Yes, I had fun with Benjamin. Yes, I think this idea of making the B&B a singles retreat is going to work."

A chorus of groans echoed in response, clearly disappointed she hadn't offered more salacious details.

Mei reached over and patted Rochelle's shoulder with a kindness that made Rochelle's chest clench. "I'm proud of you," she said, her tone gentle.

Rochelle exhaled, relaxing a fraction. Finally, they had dropped it—somewhat. But even as the conversation shifted back to the romance novel, she felt the unspoken tension swirling like a silent undercurrent. They wanted her to say more.

Truth be told, part of her wanted to say more, too, but she swallowed the impulse.

If these women thought she'd put her heart on display for them, they were out of their minds. She'd endured heartbreak before; she wasn't about to go through it again so easily.

Rochelle turned a page in her novel, eyes flicking across the text without fully absorbing the words. Deep down, she knew the truth.

Benjamin Walters was dangerous to her heart.

And she simply couldn't afford to let it break again.

CHAPTER SIXTEEN

I t isn't a date.
Nothing they had done could technically count as such, but yet, still—Benjamin had gone all out.

He fluffed a small pillow on the sofa and cast another glance at the door. Tonight's meeting should have started five minutes ago. Rochelle had texted earlier to confirm she was coming, and they had plenty of work to do.

To set the right mood—not *for a date*, but for *work*, of course—he had switched out the red pillows for blue ones, dimmed the lights just enough to feel warm but not too dark for reading, and even picked up a few scented candles for the coffee table. A subtle citrus-vanilla scent curled through the air, filling the room with a quiet sort of comfort.

Benjamin knelt in front of the sound system, wincing as his knees protested the movement. "Let's see..." he muttered, pressing a button to power up the stereo.

These days, young folks streamed music, but he still had a soft spot for the physical copies of albums he had collected over the years. A jazz queen from back in the day, one of Ilene's favorites, was already in the player. Something told him Rochelle might appreciate her, too.

As the music rolled in low and steady, he settled back onto the couch. The coffee table held a small spread—some almonds, a bottle of orange juice, and two glasses. The work ahead would be demanding, and they'd need fuel.

Then—*knock, knock, knock!*

Benjamin pushed to his feet, limping slightly. *Shouldn't have knelt like that.*

When he opened the door, Rochelle stood outside, laptop tucked under one arm, a beanie pulled snug over her head. The baby blue knit softened her usual sharp presence, making her eyes seem even brighter beneath the glow of the porch light.

"Ben!" She exhaled like she had been rushing. "So *sorry* I'm late. We said eight o'clock, and yet, here I am at *eight-ten.*" She breezed inside, pausing just long enough to inhale deeply. *"Would you look at that?"*

She sniffed the air dramatically, a playful twinkle in her eyes. "You *sure* know how to make a place feel nice."

Benjamin scratched the back of his head as she took a seat. "Just wanted us both to be comfortable while we worked."

Rochelle wasted no time booting up her laptop. "That sure was nice of you. Because *heaven knows* we're gonna be here a few hours." She sighed, but it didn't deflate her. Instead, she looked at him with that familiar, teasing spark. "Might as well enjoy the ambiance while we can."

She trailed off suddenly, her gaze drifting toward the stereo.

Benjamin's chest tightened. "Everything alright?"

A slow, nostalgic smile spread across her face. "My sister loved this song."

Then, to his surprise, she started snapping her fingers, swaying lightly, and—before he could even process it—singing along.

Benjamin chuckled, the warmth in his chest growing. "Is that so?"

The moment felt too perfect not to join in. So he did. Their voices wove together, neither of them professional vocalists, but somehow, *it didn't matter.*

When Rochelle pointed at him on a lyric that said *you*, he played along, clutching his chest dramatically.

They carried on like that, singing and laughing until their sides hurt, before finally settling down, Rochelle wiping at the corners of her eyes.

Benjamin pressed a hand to his knee as Rochelle started typing. *Lord, he loved her laugh.* It was the kind of sound that could birth angels in another universe.

"Alright," she declared. "What ideas do we have?"

He scooted a little closer. "Well, for starters, I have no doubt you've been sitting on some *brilliant* ones."

"You *know* I have." Rochelle adjusted her glasses, the glow of the screen illuminating her face. Then, she launched into it, rattling off matchmaking packages, marketing strategies, and all the ways they could bring their vision to life.

Benjamin listened intently, voicing his agreement or raising questions where necessary. There wasn't much he disagreed with—Rochelle *knew* their audience.

"That package alone should be *at least* a hundred dollars a night," he remarked.

"Of *course!*" Rochelle typed in the price with conviction. "We're not running this baby for *free*, Ben. People need to *know* this is a premium experience." She rubbed her fingers together, mimicking the universal gesture for money.

Benjamin chuckled, but his focus was slipping.

He wasn't thinking about pricing anymore.

He was thinking about *her*.

How often did a person become *inspired* just by someone else *being?* By the way they spoke, the way they moved, the way they *loved* what they did?

His mouth felt dry as he considered his next move.

It was time she knew.

Surely, by now, she must have caught on. Hadn't she noticed the way he always found reasons to see her? How quickly he had agreed to this "test run"? How he *always* complimented her?

She had to have put the pieces together.

Still—Rochelle had never *said* anything outright.

Maybe if *he* confessed first, it would inspire her to open up.

Or—at the very least—it would confirm whether his instincts were right.

Rochelle hit *enter* on her keyboard. "There we go. The bundles and specials are looking good." She skimmed the screen. "What else can we add?"

She looked at him.

Benjamin just *smiled*.

Rochelle's brow arched. "What's going on with you, Ben?" She laughed, her brows crinkling in amusement.

"Have I ever told you how much I admire the way you do things?"

She scoffed, flicking an imaginary speck of dust off her shoulder. "You *could* stand to mention it more."

Benjamin chuckled softly, but then, his expression turned serious.

"No, Rochelle. I don't mean it like that."

Her teasing halted.

"I don't mean it as a friend realizing how much his friend means to him." He leaned slightly closer. "It's *more* than that."

Rochelle's face softened. "...Oh?"

He exhaled. "It's the way you *live* life. You're exuberant. Passionate. You *love* everything you do, and that energy is *infectious*." His heart pounded. "That's why this town loves you. That's why so many people *support* you. It's why *I* support you."

He let his gaze drift toward the kitchen—toward the stove.

"Who would've thought a simple inconvenience would lead me to the woman I *want* to spend all my time with?"

Rochelle followed his gaze, and for a long moment, she didn't speak.

Benjamin smiled wistfully. "The stove broke, and I needed a new one. The replacement got delayed. I got tired of eating microwavable food." He let out a quiet chuckle. "So, I decided to eat out."

He turned back to her.

Rochelle faced him fully now, her expression unreadable.

"And when I saw you at the diner that first day—greeting customers, making *everyone* feel like family... *I never wanted to leave.*"

The smile that stretched her lips now was different. *Softer.*

Benjamin inhaled. "Getting to know you these past months has only solidified what I already knew." He searched her eyes. "I *like* you, Rochelle. *A lot.*"

Her breath hitched.

"I want to take you out. I want you to dress up and have dinner with me. I want us to go on *real* dates—picnics, walks, just... *more.*" His voice was steady. "But only if *you* want to. If you feel like exploring this, too."

Silence fell.

The insertion point on her screen blinked. The entire room had never felt *this* still.

Then—*she hummed.*

Benjamin swallowed, watching her carefully.

Her sigh was long. And heavy.

His toes curled inside his shoes.

Then, finally—she spoke.

And it was *not* what he was expecting.

CHAPTER SEVENTEEN

"*It's better to have loved and lost than never to have loved at all.*"

They never tell you how much that *loss* can consume you. How it lingers, gnawing at the edges of your peace. How it makes every step forward feel like a battle against your own mind.

Frozen.

That was how Rochelle felt now that Benjamin had laid his heart bare. Like she was trapped in some unmoving place between *denial* and *relief*.

Denial—because she didn't *want* to believe he saw her this way.

Relief—because he *did*.

Mei had been right all along. Rochelle just couldn't bring herself to say it out loud. *I am in denial.*

Denial that she had hung onto every word he spoke like it was an anchor, keeping her from drifting into the unknown.

Denial that she had felt the *exact same way* when he had first walked into her diner. The pleasant demeanor, the easy smile, the warmth in his voice—he had melted something inside her without even trying. She had felt that rush up her spine, that telltale quickening of her pulse, the way her breath had caught in her throat.

And she had ignored it.

She had been ignoring it *this whole time.*

But now—*now*—he had laid it all out. There was no more hiding from it. No more dismissing it. The question was, *what was she supposed to do with it?*

Her lip quivered as she chewed it, the silence between them growing unbearably thick. If a pin dropped now, it would *shatter* the moment like glass.

She should be saying something—anything.

But how did she tell him that after *years* of guarding herself, of focusing only on her business, on Malachi, on anything *but* her own heart, she *couldn't* let this happen?

Her heart had been broken once before, and she knew—*knew*—it couldn't survive another.

She swallowed hard.

"Ben."

Her own voice sounded foreign in the thick quiet.

He looked at her, eyes steady.

"I'm really glad that you feel that way." She forced a small, sad smile. "Flattered, too. But..." She exhaled shakily, looking straight into his eyes.

And it *crushed her.*

The way the light in them dimmed, like a storm cloud rolling over a bright summer day.

One thing Rochelle wasn't was a liar.

She had always prided herself on telling the truth, even when it was hard, even when it hurt. She had lectured Malachi about honesty, had *demanded* it from her friends, had built her life on the foundation that *truth was the only way forward.*

So she had to be honest with him now.

"…Although I do like you, too," she admitted, reaching for his hand. His palm was warm, steady, *safe*. "I can't explore this."

His fingers twitched beneath hers, and she felt the moment he processed her words.

Felt the *confusion* settle into his bones.

Benjamin turned slightly toward her, brows furrowed. "Why?" His voice was gentle, not demanding—just searching. "You *like* me too, but you won't give it a chance? I don't understand."

Rochelle felt her chest constrict.

"I know you don't," she whispered. "And you have a right not to. But I *can't* let myself get caught up in heartbreak again."

Benjamin's eyes softened. "Ms. Rochelle…" He turned his hand over, holding hers properly now, squeezing lightly. "Who says I'll break your heart?"

She yanked her hand away and shot to her feet, retreating into the kitchen like a cornered animal. She needed *space*. Distance. Anything to stop the memories clawing their way to the surface.

Brian. His voice, his demands, the way he had slowly chipped away at her sense of self. The way she had *let him*.

"No one," she admitted. But she couldn't shake the way fear curled around her like a noose.

Benjamin stood slowly, cautiously. "Then why do you assume I will? Because of *one* bad relationship?" He sighed, shoulders sinking. "Rochelle, Brian didn't know a thing about love. He was nothing but an insecure fool looking for a good time. I know what it *really* means to be there for someone. I've *done it before*. And I *want* to do it again."

He took a slow step forward.

Rochelle's back hit the chair behind her, stopping her retreat.

Benjamin reached out instinctively, steadying her. "Be careful."

Rochelle let out a shaky breath.

She felt *ridiculous*. Embarrassed. *Cowardly.*

She covered her face with her hands. "What am I doing?"

She *hated* running like this. She had never been the type. But here she was, backing away from the *kindest man she had ever known.*

Benjamin stayed where he was, watching her carefully. "Rochelle… what did you promise yourself back then?"

Her hands dropped to her sides.

"That I would never let someone break me again."

His face twisted in something like grief. "And you think *I* would break you?"

She hesitated.

He took another step closer. "If you're constantly waiting for something to end, then you're experiencing it *wrong*. Have you lived your life waiting to *die?*"

Rochelle's breath hitched.

No.

She had *lived* every single day to its fullest, had chased every passion, had thrown herself into every challenge.

So why… *why* was she treating love like something to run from?

The heat of Benjamin's presence was near now, but he didn't crowd her. He let her have space. Let her make the next move.

She shook her head slowly.

"Then why enter a relationship *waiting for the end?*" His voice was soft, almost pleading. He reached for her hand.

And this time—this time—she let him take it.

She squeezed his fingers.

"Benjy," she whispered.

He stilled.

Rochelle took a deep breath. "I *do* want this." Her voice wavered. "I want to see what we can be. I *like* you. But I'm just a mess."

"I know," he murmured. "It's what you just told me."

"No." She shook her head. "What I'm *trying* to say now is that I take it all *back*—because I *do* want to try this."

Benjamin blinked, startled. "Really?"

She nodded.

He searched her face. "Are you *sure*?"

"Yes."

His expression was unreadable. "You changed your mind... just like that?"

Rochelle sighed, walking past him to sink onto the couch. "Benjy, I *always* wanted to date you." She picked up her laptop, staring at the blank screen. "It was just *hard* to let myself *accept* it."

Benjamin moved toward her slowly, sitting beside her with a weight that made the cushions sink.

He studied her carefully. "So what changed your mind?"

Rochelle finally looked at him, meeting his steady gaze.

"What you *should* be asking," she said with a small, knowing smile, "is why I didn't just say *yes* in the first place."

Benjamin chuckled, shaking his head. "Ms. Rochelle, you make my head spin."

She laughed softly. "I make *my own* head spin."

She reached out, nudging his arm.

"You should know, Benjy," she admitted, voice softer than before. "From the moment you first walked into my diner, I *liked you.*"

Benjamin's brows lifted.

"I knew it the second I saw you." She smiled wistfully. "You sat down, and it felt like... like someone turned on a *light* in my life."

Benjamin's hand settled over hers.

"Then let's see where this light takes us," he murmured.

Rochelle squeezed his fingers.

For the first time in years, she was ready.

CHAPTER EIGHTEEN

Benjamin stepped into the diner, momentarily pausing just inside the door so the soft jingle of the bell wouldn't swallow his greeting. The aroma of fresh-brewed coffee drifted around him, mingling with the lingering scent of maple syrup and fried batter. The breakfast rush had trickled off; only a few patrons remained, quietly enjoying the slower pace. This lull was exactly what he'd counted on.

He inhaled a steadying breath. Rochelle never came in this early—she was more of a mid-morning presence these days, a routine he'd studied closely. And that gave him the perfect window to find Aimee alone, away from curious eyes and well-meaning busybodies.

But as he strode farther into the diner, Benjamin spotted not just Aimee at the counter, but also Malachi. He should've guessed the two would be together; if there was one constant in Sweetgum, it was how inseparable those two had become.

"Good morning, Ms. Aimee, Mr. Malachi." Benjamin slid onto one of the rotating stools, trying not to fidget. Despite his casual tone, an undercurrent of excitement—or maybe nerves—

coursed through him. His hands felt a bit clammy; he had to force them to stay still in his lap.

Malachi shot him a grin. "Sir, I gotta tell you—I didn't think it was possible."

Benjamin arched a brow, adjusting the front of his collar. "That being?"

Aimee practically bounced on her tiptoes, dark eyes sparkling. "Convincing Rochelle to admit she liked you and agree to a real date this afternoon." She leaned forward, pressing her palm to her heart. "We are so happy for her. She deserves someone who sees how special she is, and we know you'll treat her right."

A pleasant warmth spread through Benjamin's chest. Hearing Rochelle's family talk so openly about her well-being reminded him of how deeply she was loved—and it only intensified his resolve to do right by her. "She told you about last night?" he asked, half-wondering just how much Rochelle might have shared.

Malachi snorted. "Not directly. Mrs. Zhang apparently found out, and—well, you know how it goes. Everyone else in town got the news by dinnertime." He cast Benjamin a sympathetic smirk. "Small town living."

Benjamin blinked. "So… the whole town knows about us having a date? Already?"

Aimee nodded. "Pretty much." She reached for her notepad. "Did you come in for breakfast, or are you hoping to catch Rochelle before your date?"

Benjamin shook his head, exhaling. "Neither. I actually came to ask you for a favor."

Aimee stilled, her pen hovering. "Oh?"

Benjamin cleared his throat, slipping his phone out of his pocket. His fingers were trembling ever so slightly. He tapped the screen, then handed it to her. "I was, um, wondering if you could make *this* for our date."

Aimee's eyes went wide. "You want me to *cook* for your first official date?" She cradled the phone like it was a rare treasure. "Benjamin, that's so romantic."

Malachi leaned over to peek at the recipe. "Gumbo, huh?" He nodded in approval. "Sounds like you've been paying attention to Aunt Rochelle's favorite dishes. She'll be *so* excited."

Benjamin let out a quiet sigh of relief. "I just... want this to be special. She deserves nothing less."

Aimee was already jotting down a list of ingredients. "You got it. I'll call you as soon as it's ready." She grinned. "You set everything up, and I'll provide the food for your big night."

He offered a grateful smile. "Thank you. Truly."

When he stepped outside, the daylight flooding through the diner's windows felt impossibly bright. His stomach fluttered with hope—and a dash of anxiety. **Tonight** had to be perfect. Rochelle had known heartbreak before, and if there was any chance he could show her she was worthy of deep, unwavering love, he'd do it.

Clutching his phone, he inhaled deeply, mentally rehearsing each detail: the greenhouse, the table setting, the meal from Aimee—every puzzle piece designed to show Rochelle exactly what she meant to him.

"ALL THIS SUSPENSE is making me nervous." Rochelle's voice held a teasing edge, but Benjamin sensed genuine curiosity beneath it. Her arm looped through his in a comfortable gesture that sent warmth skittering across his skin.

He guided her along the narrow path, aware of each damp patch of earth beneath their shoes. Most of the winter's snow had melted now, leaving behind a rich smell of wet soil. Sunlight glanced off a nearby window, bright enough to make them both squint.

"Surprises can be fun," Benjamin replied, patting her hand. He tried to contain the sheer rush of contentment he felt whenever they were this close. "Just trust me."

Rochelle huffed, though amusement gleamed in her eyes. "I *do* trust you. But I also like *knowing* things, so if this is another one of your test dates, you'd better—"

"Alright, alright." He chuckled. "We're here."

They halted before the greenhouse door, its frosted glass reflecting afternoon light in dazzling shards. Benjamin gently placed a red silk tie over Rochelle's eyes, adjusting it so she couldn't peek. "Mind your step."

She let out a small squeak of protest. "Benjamin Walters, if I trip and break something—"

He covered her hand with his. "I'd never let you fall," he said quietly. Then, placing one hand at the small of her back, he guided her inside.

The air in the greenhouse was warmer, slightly humid, scented with thriving greenery. A soft rustle echoed as their coats brushed against broad leaves. Once they reached the center, he stopped, heartbeat thrumming. "Alright. Time to see."

Rochelle pulled the silky blindfold away, blinking to adjust her eyes to the filtered sunlight. As comprehension dawned, she let out a gentle, breathy laugh. "Oh… my."

Benjamin felt a surge of gratitude at her reaction. He'd spent hours arranging a small wooden table in the middle, draped in a deep red cloth that offset the greens and bursts of floral color around them. A single rose stood in a slim vase, along with plates meticulously set with silver cutlery. The gumbo pot sat on a hot plate, steam rising in savory swirls.

Even the potted blooms seemed to perk up in Rochelle's presence—a rainbow of petals forming a living curtain around them.

"Benjamin," she whispered, stepping closer to the table. Her fingertips trailed over a bright daisy, then grazed the edge of the gumbo pot, where the aroma of Creole spices and onions mingled in the air. "I've never had anyone do something like this for me."

He pulled out her chair, aware of how her expression revealed a mix of awe and an emotion he couldn't quite name. "That's because you haven't had anyone who understood how remarkable you are," he said quietly. "And that ends now."

A spark of delight lit her features, although she looked briefly uncertain about what to say next. "Flattery, huh? I see how you operate."

He laughed softly, seating her with care. "If it works, I'll keep it up." In one smooth motion, he lifted the lid on the pot, releasing a curl of fragrant steam. The spicy, savory smell surrounded them both. "Shall we?"

She grabbed her spoon, eyes shining with excitement. "Absolutely."

Benjamin dished up generous helpings of gumbo, complete with fluffy rice and crusty bread Aimee had packed. He watched Rochelle take her first bite, letting her eyes briefly close to savor the bold flavors. His entire body felt tense, waiting for her verdict.

Finally, she let out a satisfied hum. "Mmm. Aimee definitely knows what she's doing."

He chuckled, letting out a breath he hadn't realized he was holding. "I'm glad you like it."

They ate in contented silence for a moment, the clink of silverware mingling with the soft hush of the greenhouse. Rochelle peppered the meal with stories about Malachi's antics and a few nostalgic tales of Sweetgum's past. Benjamin found himself hanging on every word—each snippet of her life felt like a gateway to understanding more of who she was.

When their plates were nearly cleared, Rochelle rose, curiosity guiding her around the greenhouse's perimeter. Her gaze roamed over the vines climbing the glass walls and the budding flowers. "This place," she murmured, running a hand lightly over the leaves of a potted plant, "it's something special."

Benjamin joined her, inhaling the scent of moist earth and blossoms. "Ilene built it. I've tried to keep it close to how she left it, but it's become *our* space in a way—a piece of the B&B that still grows."

Rochelle turned, and her hand brushed his forearm. She studied him for a moment, eyes reflecting a gentle swirl of emotions. "It feels like renewal. Like no matter what's gone before, something fresh can bloom here."

Benjamin's breath hitched. "You said it better than I ever could."

They stood in silence, the quiet hum of greenhouse life filling the background. Then, cautiously, he slid his hand along hers, intertwining their fingers. The warmth of her palm against his sent an electric thrill through him.

"I'm grateful for this," he said. "For you."

She parted her lips, maybe to tease him, or to confess whatever thoughts flickered behind her gaze. But she didn't speak. Instead, she rose on her toes just enough that he felt the softness of her breath near his cheek.

Time seemed to slow. He leaned in, meeting her halfway. Their lips brushed in a gentle, unhurried kiss that stirred every part of him. It was over in a moment, yet somehow it felt timeless.

When they separated, Rochelle's eyes reflected a bright, tender look. "That's... one way to say thank you," she whispered, her voice laced with a shy humor.

Benjamin laughed, relief and joy coiling tight in his chest. "I'd do it again if it means you'll stay a moment longer."

She shook her head, but her smile was wide. "It just might." Then her gaze flicked to the greenhouse door, the late-afternoon light dancing across her expression. "We should head out soon, though, before it gets dark. You *are* walking me home, right?"

He extended his arm, adopting a mock-serious bow. "It would be my honor, Ms. Rochelle."

She looped her arm through his, stepping back into the cool, golden-hour air. A gentle wind rustled nearby branches, carrying hints of early spring. They walked side by side, careful to avoid small puddles, as the sun sank behind Sweetgum's rooftops.

Beneath the hush of evening, Benjamin felt Rochelle's presence like a promise—one that hinted at new seasons, new life, and the chance for love to thrive in places he once feared it never would again.

Yes, this was only the beginning.

CHAPTER NINETEEN

The night air carried the scent of jasmine and damp earth, lingering in the gentle hush enveloping Sweetgum's streets. Every so often, a quiet breeze rustled through the trees, bringing with it the faint sound of wind chimes from a distant porch. Rochelle had always loved how her town seemed alive even in darkness—each house sheltering its own stories, each quiet road leading to some new chapter. Tonight, though, she wasn't thinking about Sweetgum's stories.

She was thinking about hers.

And about the man walking beside her.

Benjamin's hand brushed hers—just lightly, a whisper of contact. He didn't take it outright. Didn't rush. Instead, he let the space between them bristle with a quiet, expectant energy, like a melody poised right before the chorus swells. Rochelle exhaled, watching the faint mist of her breath dissolve into the cool air.

"This is real," she murmured without fully realizing she'd spoken aloud—until she felt the slightest shift in Benjamin's stride.

"What is?" he asked gently, turning his head toward her.

She hesitated, drawing in a slow breath. "Us."

He missed a step—just barely. But she caught it. Beneath the soft amber glow of the streetlamps, his smile lifted, a subtle curve that revealed more than words could.

"It is," he confirmed quietly.

And then—finally—he closed the space between them, his fingers slipping through hers in a way that felt deliberate and sure. There was warmth in that brief, easy interlacing of hands, a silent assurance that she wasn't alone in whatever this was becoming.

Rochelle's heart thumped an agreement she couldn't quite voice.

For so many years, she'd carefully kept herself at arm's length from kind men with easy voices. Saying "yes" to another date so soon had felt like peeling off armor she'd worn for half a lifetime—because the simple act of saying yes meant letting this happen. *Letting him in.* The thought fluttered inside her, half thrilling, half terrifying. She'd braced for heartbreak enough times to feel the old readiness rise in her chest.

But Benjamin?

Benjamin hadn't crashed into her life. He walked into it—steady, quiet, and patient, as though time was his ally and he believed in waiting for her to see him clearly.

And she did.

She squeezed his hand gently as they stepped up onto the broad wooden porch of the B&B. "You sure you don't mind me taking the reins tonight?" she asked, pulling a small key from her coat pocket.

"I wouldn't have it any other way, Ms. Rochelle," he replied, his voice low and teasing. There was a warmth in his tone that sent a pleasant ripple through her.

She rolled her eyes with mock exasperation, pushing open the front door. "Good. Because I already set everything up in the lounge. And I know you enjoy a good home-cooked meal, but I wanted to do something different this time."

A flicker of curiosity lit his gaze. "Different, huh?"

Rochelle simply led him inside, letting him hear for himself the gentle strains of jazz drifting from the record player in the lounge. The B&B's reception area was dimly lit, the hush of after-hours settling into every corner. She guided him around the corner to the once-quiet sitting area.

Where earlier that evening, Rochelle had done some redecorating.

Near the grand bay window, she'd arranged a small table with a vintage chess set. The polished mahogany pieces glimmered in the soft lamplight, already lined up in their starting positions. Beside it, a platter of fruit, cheese, and crackers sat next to a bottle of wine. Low jazz music spilled from the turntable near the fireplace—a sultry saxophone line weaving through the still air. The space practically hummed with intimate energy.

Benjamin let out a low whistle, and Rochelle caught the glint of a smile in his eyes. "Well, well, well," he said, voice laced with amusement. "Ms. Rochelle, if I didn't know better, I'd say you were trying to romance me."

She lifted her chin, affecting a bored look. "Please. I'm just ensuring you don't embarrass yourself when I wipe the floor with you in chess."

He let out a soft laugh, and the sound tugged at her in ways she couldn't quite name. "Is that a challenge?" he asked, arching a brow.

"It's a fact." Rochelle approached the table and dropped into one of the cushioned chairs, gesturing for him to do the same. "Sit down and prepare yourself, Benjy. You're about to be humbled."

Benjamin studied her for a moment—really studied her—and in the stillness, Rochelle felt an awareness settle over her, something like the hush before thunder. It was the first time in longer than she could recall that a man's gaze made her want to be seen. Truly seen.

Finally, Benjamin rounded the table and took his seat. Rolling up his sleeves, he set his elbows on the table's edge. "Alright, then," he murmured. "Let's see what you've got."

∼

"You've got to be cheating." Benjamin leaned forward, scrutinizing the chessboard as though it might reveal some hidden trick.

Rochelle let out a triumphant laugh, sliding her rook across the board. The pieces made a satisfying *click* on the polished wood. "Don't be a sore loser, sugar. I told you how this was gonna go."

He groaned, dragging a hand down his face. "Alright, I surrender. You're ruthless."

She smirked, reaching for a grape from the platter. "You're just mad I got you in check four times."

Benjamin chuckled, leaning back in his chair. "You're dangerous."

"Only now you're catching on?" She arched a brow, feeling a playful streak uncoil in her chest—one she'd nearly forgotten she had. The crisp fruit and the mellow cheese had tempered her hunger, leaving her warm and content. "It's about time."

Their banter was comfortable, yet Rochelle sensed a shift. Benjamin's expression turned thoughtful—his eyes moving in that slow, deliberate way that always made her feel more aware of every breath. She swallowed, the grape rolling between her fingertips.

Then, with a boldness that sent a trickle of heat through her, Benjamin reached across the table and gently took the grape from her hand. The brief contact of his fingertips against hers—

rough and warm—sent a flicker of longing through her. She didn't quite know what to say, so she didn't say anything at all.

He popped the grape into his mouth, his eyes steady on hers. "You're trouble, Ms. Rochelle."

The quiet assurance in his tone made her pulse thud. For a moment, she tried to force a comeback—something witty or sarcastic to keep the atmosphere breezy. Nothing came to mind. She wanted to linger in that moment, to feel the weight of his attention and let it fill the space between them.

"And what does that make you?" she finally managed, her voice tinged with feigned bravado.

Benjamin huffed a near-silent laugh, a faint tilt of his head. "Patient."

Rochelle exhaled, trying to will her heartbeat into submission. The open glass of wine on the table beckoned. She poured them each a fresh splash, ignoring the slight tremor in her hand. "Alright, then," she said, lifting her glass. "To humbling lessons."

A crooked grin shaped Benjamin's lips as he clinked his glass against hers. "To dangerous women."

Their gazes held as they sipped. Rochelle found herself acutely aware of how close they were, the curve of his hand on the glass, the slight part in his lips when he lowered his drink. She set her own glass down carefully, running her tongue over her lower lip to catch a stray drop of wine.

Benjamin's gaze flicked there—just for a moment—but the silence that followed made the air feel dense, charged. Rochelle's heart hammered, every nerve on alert, wondering if he might lean over the table and—

But he didn't. Instead, he reached across, taking her hand in a calm, deliberate gesture, his fingers lacing over hers. Warm. Reassuring.

Her pulse thundered in her ears. She didn't pull away. She couldn't. A question simmered in his eyes, something he wasn't voicing. And she wasn't sure she was ready to answer it, or even if she could.

So she just held on.

And, for the first time in what felt like ages, Rochelle gave herself permission to want something more. More than banter, more than half-told truths. More than a guarded heart. She allowed herself to feel the closeness, to lean into it.

In that stillness, while the jazz record spun another sultry tune, Rochelle realized she was no longer preparing for heartbreak. She was bracing for something else entirely—something that felt a lot like hope.

The moment Benjamin's fingers closed around hers, a quiet spark seemed to pass between them. It was subtle—no fireworks, no dramatic flourish—but the warmth that coursed through his palm and into his chest was enough to set his heart hammering. He couldn't tell if she felt it, too, but the way her gaze dropped to their joined hands made him suspect she did.

He lifted his thumb, tracing a small, deliberate circle against the back of Rochelle's hand. Her breath caught, so faint he barely registered the sound. Yet he heard it, all the same. He'd never imagined that something as simple as holding hands could carry so much meaning. And after all these years—of loneliness, of building walls around heartache—he found himself wanting to hold on to that feeling for as long as she'd let him.

Over by the record player, the sultry saxophone continued its low, haunting melody. To Benjamin, it sounded like an invitation for them to move closer. But he stayed where he was, letting Rochelle decide if she wanted to close that small space between them.

CHAPTER TWENTY

Her cheeks, usually colored by confident mischief, looked warmer under the soft lamplight. She watched him carefully, her eyes flicking over his face as though searching for reassurance. He wished he could speak volumes in that single look— tell her how much it meant to him that she was here, and how he would wait all night for her to feel safe in this closeness.

At last, Rochelle cleared her throat. "So," she said, voice a touch unsteady despite her best efforts at composure, "was that your way of saying I'm in trouble?"

A flicker of amusement eased the tightness in Benjamin's chest. He almost smiled. "I don't think you're the one who's in trouble," he teased gently. "It might be me instead."

Her brow arched slightly. "Oh? And why's that, Mr. Walters?"

Because you make me feel alive, he thought. Because I can't look at you without feeling like I'm about to lose my balance. But he simply answered with a quiet, "You're too quick for me in chess. I'm not sure if my ego can handle a second round."

She laughed then—a low, husky sound that sent a pleasant flutter through his stomach. He loved that laugh, loved the full warmth of it. In that moment, he realized he would do whatever he could to hear it more often.

"Maybe if you spent less time distracting me with those smiles, you'd have noticed my next move," she countered, chin tilting up in playful challenge.

Benjamin let his own smile spread slowly. "I'll keep that in mind for our rematch." With cautious deliberation, he guided her closer, one hand sliding along her waist. She didn't resist. Instead, she exhaled a small, shaky breath and allowed him to lead her away from the chessboard, away from the table of fruit and wine, into an open patch of floor near the fireplace.

He settled his free hand lightly on her hip, keeping the other curled around her fingers. The saxophone tune was languid— perfect for a slow dance that required neither skillful footwork nor fancy turns. Just an intimate sway that let them both feel something they hadn't dared reach for in far too long.

She dipped her head, letting her forehead hover just near his shoulder. He felt the warmth of her breath through his shirt, each exhalation sending a pulse of awareness through his nerves. For a second, he closed his eyes and breathed her in, taking note of the subtle hint of vanilla and the sharper under-current of anticipation in the air.

In that hush, he gave himself permission to want. To want this closeness, this *possibility*, with all the hope simmering in his chest.

When Rochelle finally spoke, her voice was a near whisper. "I…haven't done this in ages. Not just the dancing," she clarified, as though reading his mind, "but letting someone get this close."

Benjamin's hold on her waist tightened just a fraction, a gentle reassurance. "I haven't either," he admitted. "But some things are worth facing our fears for." He paused, aware of his heart pounding. "I think you are."

She let out a slow breath, and he felt the tension ebb from her shoulders. For a moment, neither of them spoke—words could only crowd a moment that needed no further explanation.

At length, she pulled back just enough to look into his eyes. He could see the soft reflection of the fireplace dancing in her gaze, could feel the slight tremor in her fingers where they rested against his. She looked vulnerable in a way he doubted many had seen: no razor-sharp quips, no guarded half-smiles. Just quiet openness that left her heart on display.

"Benjamin," she said softly, and in that single word, he heard both a question and a plea.

He slid one hand from her waist up to her cheek, the pad of his thumb brushing over her skin. She leaned into his touch, and a tremor of gratitude flowed through him at how willingly she let down her walls, even for an instant.

Without dropping her gaze, he bent his head, pausing just a heartbeat away from her lips. He wanted her to feel the choice was hers, that she could pull back if she needed to. But Rochelle didn't pull back. Her eyelids fluttered shut, and that was all the permission he required.

He kissed her softly, a warm, lingering press that left him dizzy at how right it felt. He sensed her sigh against his mouth, heard the faint hitch of her breath as she relaxed into him. In that electric hush, the world outside the lounge might as well have disappeared. No hustle of the street, no echoes of guests passing by—just two people who'd finally given themselves permission to *want*.

When they parted, Rochelle's eyes opened to meet his. The vulnerability still glimmered there, but so did a certainty he hadn't seen before. It stole his breath anew.

"You're not the only one in trouble," she whispered, a small, wry smile curving her lips.

Benjamin's own lips quirked upward in a grin that felt almost boyish. "Then I suppose we can be in trouble together."

She ducked her head, resting it against his shoulder. They swayed to the soft music once more, her arms slipping around his torso as though they'd always belonged there. He pressed his cheek to the top of her head, eyes closing while they rocked in tandem, each step a quiet vow not to let this moment slip away too soon.

In that stolen stretch of time, Benjamin could only think of one thing:

He didn't want to let her go. Not tonight, not anytime soon.

CHAPTER TWENTY-ONE

Rochelle held onto Benjamin as if he might vanish if she loosened her grip—an irrational but persistent fear nipping at the edges of her mind. She couldn't remember the last time she'd allowed herself to be so... *unguarded*. Yet here she was, her cheek pressed against the warm expanse of his chest, listening to the rhythmic thud of his heartbeat beneath his shirt.

They continued to sway, cocooned in the gentle glow of the fireplace and the lingering notes of the fading jazz tune. The smell of old leather chairs and that faint trace of cedar from the logs made the lounge feel snug, private—like they were the only two people in the world. With every measured step, Rochelle found it harder to deny the ache of longing fluttering low in her belly: a desire for more time, more closeness, more of *this* quiet comfort.

She lifted her face by a fraction, enough to see the outline of Benjamin's jaw and the silver hint of his stubble. "If we stay like this any longer," she murmured, her voice barely above a hush, "someone might come in thinking we've fallen asleep on our feet."

A soft chuckle rumbled through his chest. "I'd risk it," he replied, arms cinching a little tighter around her waist. "But if you prefer a change of scenery, you just say the word."

Rochelle's lips twitched into a smile. The notion of leaving his embrace felt like giving up a lifeline she'd only just found, but part of her wanted an excuse to lighten the mood before it got too intense. "We could...sit," she suggested softly, though a part of her still clung to him.

"Sit," Benjamin echoed, pulling back enough to meet her gaze.

For a moment, she simply stared, struck by how the lines on his face—evidence of laughter and time—looked so endearing under low light. She cleared her throat, easing out of his hold. "I figure if you're going to stay here in the lounge for a while, we may as well put those fruit and crackers to better use."

His eyes gleamed with something warm. "Lead the way, Ms. Rochelle."

They walked the short distance back to the small table where their abandoned chess set waited, rooks and pawns still scattered across the board from their recent spar. Rochelle lowered herself into one of the plush chairs and tried to ignore the flutter in her stomach as Benjamin took the seat beside her—close enough that his knee brushed hers beneath the table.

She scooped up a cluster of grapes, rolling one between her fingers before popping it into her mouth. The sweetness burst across her tongue, a small shock of flavor that made her realize how aware she was of every sensation tonight—sound, taste, the brush of his sleeve when he leaned forward.

"I've never lost so spectacularly in chess," Benjamin said, easing the tension with a crooked smile. His voice was pitched low, intimate in the hush of the lounge. "Honestly, I almost forgot which piece moves where."

Rochelle laughed, letting herself enjoy the playful banter. "Don't blame that on me. You said you could keep up."

His brow rose. "And it's not the first time I've bitten off more than I could chew." Then his expression softened. "But you make it worth every misstep."

Her pulse skipped. She wanted to tease him, say something that'd bring them back to safer territory, but the tenderness in his voice disarmed her. "You do realize you're making it very hard for me to keep any distance," she murmured, picking at the linen napkin on the table.

Benjamin reached over and lightly grazed the back of her hand. "Maybe I don't want you to."

A rush of emotion fluttered through Rochelle, so strong she had to look away for a moment. She remembered how fiercely she'd guarded herself against these kinds of moments—once upon a time, she'd sworn she would never again surrender to something this vulnerable. But now, she found she couldn't hold onto that resolve in front of Benjamin's calm eyes and gentle smile.

She swallowed. "What happens next, Ben?" The words left her in a quiet exhale, as though asking for permission to let herself believe in this possibility.

"Next," he said, taking her hand and lacing his fingers through hers, "we keep doing exactly this—seeing where it leads. One step at a time. No rush."

Rochelle studied their entwined hands. The corners of her eyes stung with relief she hadn't known she needed. No rush. She could handle that. "All right," she whispered, meeting his gaze at last. "One step at a time."

They settled into an easy silence. Outside, the faintest sounds of the night seeped through the windows—tree branches creaking in the breeze, an occasional car passing on the street. But in here, it felt like time itself had slowed to a contented crawl.

In a burst of courage, Rochelle reached for the wine and poured a little more into each of their glasses. Then she held up hers, tipping it in his direction. "To...to second chances," she said softly, the words feeling monumental in the small space.

Benjamin lifted his glass in return, his eyes steady on hers. "To second chances," he echoed, voice carrying the weight of every hope neither of them had dared voice aloud.

They clinked glasses. And as Rochelle sipped, feeling the pleasant warmth of the wine slide down her throat, she realized something unexpected: for the first time in ages, she wasn't scared of wanting more. She was *ready* for it.

And from the gentle, certain look Benjamin offered her, she had a feeling he was, too.

CHAPTER TWENTY-TWO

Benjamin watched Rochelle raise her glass, eyes still reflecting the tender glow of the fireplace. Moments earlier, they'd toasted to second chances, the faint chime of their glasses echoing in his chest like a promise. It amazed him how, in such a short span of time, she had managed to peel away so much of his guarded past—simply by letting him see glimpses of her own vulnerability.

He sipped his wine, the mellow flavor rolling over his tongue. Across the table, Rochelle studied him, and he could practically feel the gentle weight of her gaze. Their fingers were still linked, resting between them in a quiet show of trust.

"You seem to be in your head," she murmured, tilting her head slightly. "Anything I should know about?"

Benjamin inhaled, letting a soft half-laugh escape. "I'm just… thinking about how surreal this feels," he admitted. "I never expected to be here, with you, sharing…well, *this*."

He didn't specify *what* "this" was—he wasn't even sure he had the right word for it. Maybe it was simply the beginning of something he hadn't dared to dream possible. The corners of

Rochelle's mouth lifted, as if she understood the meaning behind his fumbling words.

"Not surreal for me," she said quietly, but there was warmth underneath her confident tone. "More like...refreshing."

Benjamin squeezed her hand, feeling a subtle jolt in his chest at the way her shoulders relaxed, as though she was finally letting some invisible weight slip off. "Refreshing, huh?" he echoed. "I guess that makes two of us."

Outside, a faint breeze rattled the old windows of the B&B lounge. The distant hum of a car passing by reminded him that life kept moving just beyond these walls. But right now, in the muted glow and the hush of this moment, Benjamin wanted to freeze time—hold this pocket of comfort and possibility forever.

He set his glass down and turned fully toward her. "So," he began, voice rumbling low, "care to make a bet on who wins our next chess rematch?"

She laughed, the sound soft yet playful. "Confident much? I think we both know who's got the sharper mind for that board." Then she paused, a gleam sparking in her eyes. "But let's say if *you* win, you get to pick our next date spot. If I win...well, I guess I get to see just how far your creativity can stretch."

He was certain she'd win—that was the funny part. But the promise of picking their next date gave him reason to try, at least. "Deal," he answered, his voice hitching with anticipation. "Though I might throw the match just to see how inventive you can be."

She rolled her eyes, reaching out to nudge his arm. "Don't you dare. I want a real challenge, Benjy."

"Fair enough." He caught her hand before it retreated, pressing a small kiss to her knuckles. The impulse was gentle yet fierce, bearing witness to the flood of tenderness he found himself feeling for her these days. "No throwing matches. Full competition mode next time."

Her playful grin faltered for just a moment, giving him a glimpse of something more serious beneath. "You know," she said softly, "I appreciate the lightness of this, but I also appreciate that you don't…push. You're letting me take it one step at a time."

Benjamin released her hand, sliding his fingers instead to rest over hers on the table. "Rochelle, I'm in no rush. We can go as slow as you need." He felt his heart squeeze at the flicker of gratitude in her gaze. "To me, spending time with you—whatever we're doing—beats any alternative."

She blinked quickly, like she was holding back a deeper reaction. "You keep saying things like that, and I'll end up expecting them every day."

A low chuckle escaped his throat. "Guess I'll just have to keep delivering, then."

Silence stretched again, thick with so many unspoken questions—questions about how they'd proceed, how much to share, how to let themselves hope for something more. In that silence, Benjamin leaned closer. Rochelle didn't flinch. Instead, she tilted her chin up, letting him see the spark of intrigue lighting her eyes. That was all the invitation he needed.

He brushed a featherlight kiss across her temple, and she let out a shaky sigh, turning her face so that her cheek rested against his lips. The contact sent a tremor of awe through him— how simple gestures could feel so significant, so *alive*.

Her voice came out as a near-whisper. "You're good at this, you know."

He could hardly find breath for words. "At what?"

"Making me…believe."

Benjamin felt a lump tighten in his throat. He grazed his thumb across the curve of her hand, wishing he had grander gestures or grander words. Instead, he settled for something true and simple. "You've given me reasons to believe, too."

Her lips curved in the faintest smile, as though content with that answer. Leaning back in her chair, Rochelle eased a long, slow breath. "Well then, Mr. Walters, how about we see if we can find some chess pieces that *aren't* scattered all over the board. I'm feeling lucky right now."

Benjamin stood, offering his hand with a flourish of gallantry. "Allow me to help, Ms. Rochelle."

She took it, rising from her seat, never letting their clasp break. *One step at a time,* he reminded himself, feeling the comfortable weight of her fingers twined in his. He'd savor every moment—because it wasn't just a game or a date anymore.

It was *them,* finding a rhythm that felt as inevitable as it was exhilarating.

CHAPTER TWENTY-THREE

Rochelle traced her fingertip along the rim of her teacup, letting the warmth seep into her hand. Even with the light chatter of other customers nearby, she felt Benjamin's presence more than she heard it—his gentle breath and the quiet shift of his chair against the floor. They'd decided to meet at a little bistro on the edge of Sweetgum, a cozy place known for fresh pastries and classical music drifting from a corner speaker. The bistro's interior was all weathered wood and floral wallpaper, painted in the memory of simpler times.

They were sharing a table by the bay window, watery sunlight spilling across their joined hands. She caught herself smiling for no reason—well, no reason beyond the fact that *he* was here, sliding his thumb in slow circles over her knuckles as if he never wanted to let go.

Benjamin glanced up from the menu, eyes crinkling in amusement. "You have that look again," he teased, voice low enough for only her to hear.

Rochelle gave him a mock frown. "What look?"

"That dreamy one. Like you're miles away—except your eyes say you're right here with me."

A pleased shiver trailed down her spine. "Maybe I just enjoy the scenery," she quipped, freeing one hand to gesture at the bistro's quaint decor. But the soft note in her voice betrayed the real meaning behind her words.

He lifted an eyebrow, a knowing smile tugging at his lips. "I see. So it's the doilies on the tables and the crocheted curtains that have you glowing like that."

She laughed, reaching out to pat his cheek in pretend scolding. "Don't get too cocky, Mr. Walters. You might lose your head if it inflates any bigger."

Beneath the playful banter, Rochelle felt her chest grow warm with affection. This closeness—this ability to tease and be teased—meant more to her than she could easily explain. For years, she'd closed herself off, convinced that letting someone in was risking heartbreak. But sitting here, on a lazy afternoon while sunlight dappled his graying hair, she realized heartbreak didn't scare her as much anymore. If it meant more hours like this—where they lingered over coffee and scones, unhurried and content—she'd risk a million broken pieces.

"So," Benjamin said, clearing his throat as he set the menu aside. "Have you thought more about the packages we're offering for the B&B's rebrand?"

Rochelle smiled into her teacup. Even their "business talk" felt personal now, every conversation nudging them closer together. "Yes. I figure we'll finalize the couples' weekend itinerary by next week, but I'd love your input on the dinner-and-dance event we're planning." She took a careful sip before adding, "You do owe me a tango rematch—remember who out-twirled you last time?"

His hand tightened around hers, a look of mock-offense shaping his features. "As I recall, you nearly toppled us both when you tried that fancy spin."

She stuck out her tongue. "You'd have me believe you didn't enjoy every second of that fiasco?"

Something in Benjamin's expression softened. "I enjoyed *every* second, Rochelle," he said, voice thick with sincerity.

The directness of it squeezed her heart, and suddenly the clink of silverware and low hum of chatter faded into a dull background hush. Rochelle lowered her gaze to their linked hands. She hadn't realized until that moment how badly she wanted to hear him say things like that—simple, honest, unadorned truths.

"Me too," she admitted softly, sliding her thumb along the back of his hand. "Every second."

They sat in comfortable silence for a few heartbeats, taking in each other's presence. Rochelle's mind drifted to the last couple of weeks: the sweet goodnight calls, the morning walks that never ended without a gentle kiss at her gate, and the laughter that came so easily whenever they were in the same room. How she'd once believed her time for such things had come and gone—it felt absurd now. She was living proof that no matter how many years had passed, joy could still appear, wrapped in a man's easygoing grin and the warmth of his gentle hands.

When the waiter approached with a grin to take their order, Rochelle nearly forgot what she'd intended to eat. She blamed Benjamin for that—how could she think of pastries when his gaze made her skin tingle?

After they'd settled on a couple of croissants and the bistro's daily special, Benjamin lifted his eyes back to her, amused. "It's a wonder we get any planning done at all," he joked. "Between your ideas and my distractions, we might never finalize the details for the B&B."

Her heart thrummed with contentment. "You're not just a distraction, you know," she said, her tone more serious than intended. "Working with you—it's...well, it's better than anything I've had in a long time."

The way his eyes flickered at her confession made her want

to kiss him right then and there. But she settled for entwining their fingers under the table, giving his palm a reassuring squeeze.

They filled the next hour with hushed talk of the B&B's upcoming launch—debating color schemes, potential activities, and the best way to incorporate local vendors. Rochelle found herself marveling at how seamlessly he worked with her, how each suggestion sparked a new idea in her mind. Their synergy felt effortless, a puzzle sliding neatly into place. All the while, he would sneak in a small compliment, or brush his thumb over her wrist, which made her grin like a love-struck teenager.

When the waiter brought their food—flaky croissants and savory soup—Benjamin handed her a fork with a flourish. "M'lady," he said, teasingly formal, "may I interest you in a taste?"

She tried not to laugh as she took the offered fork. "Stop it, you charmer. You're making me blush."

"Is that a bad thing?" He slid his own fork into a steaming bowl of soup, blowing on it gently before taking a sip.

Rochelle's heart stuttered. "No," she said, her voice turning quiet again. "No, it's not bad at all."

A sense of peace draped over them, thick like honey. She couldn't stop thinking about how his presence eased an ache she hadn't admitted was still there. Even the small talk felt charged with unspoken meaning. A few tables away, a trio of older women watched them with undisguised curiosity—probably neighbors from Sweetgum who loved good gossip. Rochelle didn't mind. Let them speculate. She wasn't ashamed of how besotted she looked.

At one point, she reached across the table to flick a stray crumb from Benjamin's chin, and he caught her wrist with gentle care, pressing a light kiss to her palm. The sweetness of that gesture had her cheeks warming for the thousandth time that day.

"Thank you for letting me in," he murmured, as though aware of the significance behind her vulnerability.

Rochelle lowered her gaze, feeling something in her chest give way—like a final barricade that no longer had a purpose. *Maybe I have been silly all these years,* she mused. *Maybe letting someone like Benjamin in isn't a risk—it's a gift I should have allowed myself long ago.*

They finished the meal with quieter conversation, each lost in the other's company. Once the check was paid, Benjamin stood and offered his arm, a habit that never failed to warm her heart. Rochelle looped her hand around his elbow, letting him guide her from the cozy bistro into the mild evening air.

Outside, twilight painted the streets in lavender shadows, and a gentle breeze ruffled the new leaves on the trees lining the road. Rochelle took in a deep breath of sweet, fresh air and smiled up at him. "Walk me home?" she asked softly, half-hoping he'd say yes and half-hoping he'd suggest a detour to lengthen their time together.

Benjamin's eyes gleamed. "Always."

And as they fell into step side by side, Rochelle realized she felt no hurry, no fear, no urge to second-guess the soft glow of contentment inside her. She was done running from the *possibility* that maybe—just maybe—this could be the real thing.

CHAPTER TWENTY-FOUR

Benjamin had never been one to rush. Life, he'd learned, had a gentle way of unfolding when given space—like a flower coaxed by sunlight, or a story that needed every page to reveal itself. The best moments, in his experience, were the ones that came to you when you were ready.

And yet, with Rochelle, he felt a kind of eager warmth that defied his usual patience.

Not impatience, exactly—he didn't want to push or hurry anything. But there was a quiet urgency humming beneath his ribs whenever she looked at him. Whenever her laugh filled the air, clear and certain. Whenever her hand slipped into his without a second thought.

It had only been a handful of weeks since they'd made their relationship official, yet it didn't feel new. It felt like a comforting presence that had always been there, waiting for the two of them to notice.

Which was why, when Rochelle called him that evening out of nowhere and asked in a calm, measured voice, "Can I come over?"—he'd said yes without a blink. No preamble. No explanation. She didn't owe him any. He wanted her here, for whatever reason she needed.

Now, the kettle on his stove began its slow whistle, signaling it was ready. Benjamin glanced at the clock on the wall. She'd be here any minute.

He had no idea if it would be a casual drop-in or if something weighed on her mind. But that didn't matter—she was welcome always.

A knock came at the door, clean and brisk. He turned off the burner, wiping his hands on a dish towel before crossing the short distance to the entrance. His heart gave a subtle flip, anticipation settling in his chest.

And there she stood.

Windblown, a little breathless, wrapped in one of those light cardigans she sometimes forgot to button properly. Her arms were crossed, holding back the late-evening chill; but her eyes held a warmth that made the whole world feel a little brighter.

"Hi," she said, her voice softer than usual.

Benjamin tilted his head, stepping to one side so she could pass. "Come in."

She didn't hesitate. The moment she crossed the threshold, he sensed a small shift in her posture—like a tension she'd been carrying all day finally lifted.

He shut the door gently, reaching to ease the cardigan from her shoulders. She let him do it without protest, her fingertips brushing his wrist for a moment before she turned, gaze drifting toward the living room. The space was softly lit by a single lamp, the rest of the house shrouded in evening shadows.

"I wasn't interrupting anything, was I?" Rochelle asked, noting the chessboard still arranged on the coffee table from their last game. The black and white pieces, half-moved, looked like they'd paused mid-battle.

Benjamin chuckled. "Just me and my tea," he said, moving

past her toward the small kitchen nook. "I've got some on if you're in the mood."

"Always," she said simply, an undercurrent of relief in her tone.

He admired that about her—the ease with which she occupied his home, settling in like she belonged. No excessive politeness or fidgeting. She just *was*. He liked that. Possibly more than he should.

In the kitchen, he poured two mugs of steaming tea, inhaling the floral scent that curled into the air. When he returned, Rochelle had tucked herself into the corner of the couch, legs drawn beneath her. She stared through the window at the last glow of twilight, a pensive look resting on her features.

Benjamin handed her the tea, their fingers touching briefly. Her murmured thanks was quiet, intimate in the soft hush of the room. For a moment, they just sat: two cups, two gentle sips, and the hush of wind pressing against the windows, like it was testing the house's warmth.

Finally, in a voice so low he almost missed it, Rochelle spoke. "I was thinking about my sister today."

Benjamin shifted his attention to her, noticing how she continued to watch the steam swirl above her cup. He said nothing at first, only set his own mug aside, letting the crackle of the nearby heater fill the silence.

Rochelle went on, voice calm yet tinged with old echoes of loss. "I'm not sure why. It's not an anniversary or anything. Just… she was on my mind."

Benjamin let the moment settle before he responded. "Grief's funny like that."

She huffed a quiet laugh. "Yeah." A small sigh left her lips as she turned the mug in her hands. "It used to scare me, you know? How I could go for days—weeks—without thinking about her, and then suddenly, she's everywhere. I felt guilty for letting time pass like that, for not holding on tight."

He nodded, remembering a time when he'd wrestled the same guilt about Ilene. "I know exactly what you mean."

That made Rochelle glance at him, really look this time. "And now? Does it still...?"

Benjamin steadied himself, finding the words to fit the shape of his memories. "Now, I think of Ilene when I choose to—or when something reminds me. It doesn't feel like a punch in the gut anymore." He paused, then offered a small, thoughtful shrug. "More like... a visit."

She seemed to soak that in, then nodded. "A visit," she repeated quietly. "I like that."

They lapsed back into silence, but it was comfortable. A shared solace that needed no immediate conversation. Benjamin took a slow sip of tea, letting the warmth spread through him as the moment stretched gently.

Rochelle shifted, setting her mug on the low table. Her expression softened; a hint of decision flickered in her eyes. Then she scooted closer, settling against his side, letting her head rest on his shoulder.

Benjamin inhaled, not out of shock but out of something like reverence. He raised his arm, draping it lightly across her back. It was a quiet, tentative gesture, as though asking permission without words. She exhaled softly, nestling a bit more firmly against him.

And in that simple contact, he felt the subtle power of what they shared—a bond that required no explanations or apologies. He didn't need to speak any grand declarations tonight. Rochelle didn't need to offer any, either. They were just... present, holding onto each other's nearness.

The steady rhythm of her breathing filled him with a gentle ache he recognized as hope.

Yes, he thought, he knew what this was, what it was growing into. He didn't have to push or rush. The time would come when they'd put it all into words.

CHAPTER TWENTY-FOUR

For now, the quiet was enough.

He felt Rochelle relax even further, releasing a tension she might not have known she was carrying. A faint whoosh from the heater broke the hush, the warm air caressing them both, making the house feel cocooned against the dark outside.

Benjamin closed his eyes briefly, savoring the moment. Yes, he knew. And maybe, just maybe—

She did, too.

CHAPTER TWENTY-FIVE

Rochelle never really considered forever. Not for herself, anyway. She'd once believed forever was reserved for women whose lives were just beginning—young hearts fluttering with possibilities, their biggest worries a question of when to settle down rather than if. She'd been that woman, once upon a time, full of wide-eyed wonder and irrepressible hope.

But then life got in the way.

She'd tucked away that sense of unlimited time the day loss found her—through responsibilities that demanded she stop dreaming and start doing, and more quietly, through the gradual acceptance that some doors close, never to be opened again. She loved fiercely where she could: Malachi, the diner, her friends. She cared in all the ways that mattered. But as for committing her heart—giving someone the promise of a future? That felt like a luxury her younger self had taken for granted.

Right until now.

Tonight, everything seemed different. Her pulse thrummed at the base of her throat as she climbed the wooden steps to Benjamin's porch. A gentle wind carried the faint scent of magnolia and early evening dew, curling around her ankles in a soft hush. Ordinarily, that hush would lull her. But tonight, her mind buzzed with a realization that flickered like a neon sign in the dark:

She wanted more.

She wanted the peace of sharing a warm meal with Benjamin, the routine of checking in on him, the small miracles hidden in everyday life—like hearing his gentle hum from the kitchen or being on the receiving end of his quiet, steady smiles. She wanted to gather all these little moments into a tapestry that might, if she dared, stretch all the way into forever.

Her palm still tingled with the ghost of his touch from earlier that afternoon. They'd only brushed hands when passing each other in the hallway—just that small, unassuming brush of fingers—but it had been enough to send a spark up her arm that refused to leave.

Rochelle paused at the top step, inhaling deeply. She forced herself to take a steadying breath before giving a soft knock, then another.

No answer.

Well, he'd told her more than once she never needed to knock. That, in his words, "You're always welcome, Ms. Rochelle. No knocking needed." She'd argued at the time that even close friends needed to respect each other's space, but that invitation still lodged itself in her heart, making her feel safe in a way she hadn't realized she craved.

She turned the doorknob gently, hearing it click open. A wave of warmth lapped against her like a welcoming tide—somewhere between the faint smell of cinnamon and the unmistakable heat of a low-burning fire. The living room lamp shed a cozy glow across worn-but-inviting furniture. An empty mug perched on the edge of the coffee table, a folded newspaper placed neatly beside it.

Benjamin wasn't there, but soft shuffling sounds drifted

from the nearby kitchen—an undercurrent of something simmering, the faint metallic scrape of a spoon on a pot. Rochelle's heart thrummed once more. She never knew cooking could sound so comforting, but with Benjamin, it did.

She made her way across the living room, her footsteps muffled on the plush rug. With each step, she took in the small details that gave his home a sense of history: the framed photographs on the mantel, the crocheted blanket folded at the sofa's edge, the shallow indent on the recliner that hinted at countless nights spent reading or dozing by the fire.

In the kitchen, Benjamin stood at the stove, his broad back turned. His sweater sleeves were bunched at the elbows, revealing forearms that flexed every time he stirred. An old tune she didn't quite recognize rumbled under his breath—a baritone hum that vibrated softly in the warm air.

Seeing him so at ease, so in his element, made Rochelle's chest feel tight. Could she really be undone by the sight of a man stirring soup? It seemed absurd. And yet her stomach fluttered with a mix of delight and nerves.

She cleared her throat. "You always cook like you're expecting company?"

He turned with a smile that was gentle, unhurried—one that warmed his dark eyes and made them crinkle at the corners. "Only when I like the company," he said.

That sparkle in his gaze sent a pulse of heat through her. She tried for a droll eye-roll, ignoring the dancing feeling in her stomach. "That better not be that heavy stew you tried to feed me last time. I thought I'd need a wheelbarrow to roll myself out of here afterward."

A husky chuckle rolled from his chest, and he tapped the wooden spoon lightly against the pot's rim. "You underestimate me," he teased, lifting the spoon toward her in invitation. "Gumbo tonight. Different, I promise."

Rochelle took a step closer, letting him guide the spoon to

her lips. The moment the hot, rich flavor met her tongue, her eyes fluttered shut in a reflexive sigh of pleasure. A medley of spices—paprika, cayenne, onion—mixed with something indescribably comforting.

"Oh," she murmured after swallowing, eyes still closed.

Benjamin's laugh was like a low chord in her ears, deep and resonant. "That good?"

"That good," she confirmed, carefully licking a stray drop of broth from her bottom lip. When she opened her eyes, she caught him watching her, his expression quiet and intent.

In the space between heartbeats, time seemed to slow. His gaze made her feel as if every aspect of her—every twitch, every breath—was fully seen. It should have made her uneasy; in the past, that kind of scrutiny might have sent her heart slamming up barricades. Instead, she felt calm, safe, and… wanted.

She quickly stepped back before the moment tightened into something that might force words out of her she wasn't yet ready to say. "Alright, you win," she declared with forced breeziness, turning to grab two bowls from the overhead cabinet. "You've officially cooked something I can't complain about."

He placed a hand to his chest, feigning relief. "I'll take that as the highest praise, Ms. Rochelle."

A little breath of laughter escaped her as she set the bowls on the counter. She'd been in this kitchen enough times that the cupboards felt like second nature—she found the spoons, the ladle, all without needing to ask. And each time she reached for something, she found him near, a steady presence at her side, or just behind her.

His fingers grazed her back as she shifted to ladle out the gumbo. That faint, ghosting touch—so natural, so unassuming —sent a flutter up her spine. The same question spun in her mind: *Am I really ready for this?*

His quiet attentiveness was a reminder of how carefully he treated her. He wasn't rushing. He wasn't pushing. He was there, just within reach, waiting for her to decide exactly how far she wanted him to step into her life.

And Rochelle realized then, maybe for the first time, that he'd been doing that all along—waiting. Standing there with open arms, letting her call the shots, letting her define the pace. She sensed he could see more of her than she wanted to admit: the hidden fears, the lingering grief. Yet he never demanded anything. He simply... stayed.

Carrying both brimming bowls, Rochelle moved toward the small table in the corner—near a window that overlooked his back porch. The star-flecked sky beyond glowed with possibilities she'd once assumed were behind her. Now, she wondered if those possibilities might be shining right here in front of her.

Benjamin followed with a loaf of crusty bread on a cutting board, that easy smile playing around his mouth. "If this gumbo doesn't do the trick," he joked quietly, "I don't know what else might convince you of my cooking chops."

She smirked, setting the bowls down. "You say that like I'm hard to impress."

He angled his head. "Aren't you?"

Her lips parted to protest, but then she caught the wry amusement in his eyes. She found herself laughing, shaking her head while he pulled out a chair for her. "Oh, hush," she murmured, easing into the seat he offered.

He circled to his own chair and sank down, resting his forearms on the table. The overhead light cast a warm glow across the planes of his face, highlighting the gentle lines at the corners of his eyes—lines from years of living, from sorrow and from smiles. Rochelle wondered briefly what it would be like to memorize every one of them, to trace them until they were as familiar as her own reflection.

She took her first proper spoonful of gumbo, letting the flavors dance on her tongue. Warmth bloomed in her chest, and it wasn't only from the food. The idea of eating a shared meal here, again and again, flickered in her mind like a movie reel—her pulling ingredients from the fridge, him tinkering with spices, them drifting around the kitchen in a well-worn dance.

It sounded domestic. It sounded… permanent.

Was that so wrong to want?

She glanced at Benjamin. He was watching her from across the table, the same comforting patience in his expression. Only now, she noticed the hints of anticipation around his eyes—like he could sense the turn of her thoughts, sense that her heart was shifting in ways she hadn't admitted aloud.

He didn't speak, and she didn't force herself to fill the silence. Instead, she let her mind roam through the memories they'd built: the late-night planning sessions for the B&B, the low-lit dances they'd shared in the lounge, the playful banter over chess, the stolen glances that became harder and harder to ignore.

Rochelle set her spoon aside, swallowing a sudden surge of emotion. She could say it now. She could open her mouth, tell him she wanted forever. That she was ready—maybe not fearless, but ready.

But she didn't.

Not yet. Some words merited their own space, needed time to settle in the air. She wanted to choose just the right moment, the right breath, to tell him that the life she'd never expected to be hers—full of second chances and everyday joys—was exactly the life she wanted now, with him.

So she just slid her foot under the table, pressing her ankle lightly against his in an unspoken promise. He glanced down, a flicker of curiosity in his eyes, then smiled with soft realization.

She offered him a lazy grin, letting the tension in her chest unravel. "You know," she said, aiming for casual, "you're not the worst company I've kept."

He huffed a small laugh, feigning offense. "High praise from you, Ms. Rochelle."

"Don't get cocky. I might just be complimenting the gumbo."

A warm glimmer returned to his gaze. "I'd hate to think you only come around for the food."

Her chest tightened—not painfully, but with a jolt of feeling she could barely contain. "Maybe I'll let you wonder a bit longer," she teased, managing a soft laugh.

But she knew the truth. She wasn't here for the gumbo, or for the cozy living room, or even for the chance to offer him marketing help. She was here for him—and the long, open road that stretched before them, a road she was no longer afraid to walk.

She breathed in the scent of cinnamon and simmering spices, letting the moment settle. Her chest felt brimming, but in a good way, like she was finally ready to hold more than she ever thought possible.

Soon, she promised herself. She'd find the right words, wrap them in truth, and offer them to him, hoping he'd take them and hold them safe. Because Benjamin was worth that risk.

For now, she allowed the quiet comfort of the evening to cradle them both. He gave her a knowing smile, one that told her he could wait as long as she needed.

And Rochelle—her heart still knocking with anticipation—realized she wasn't afraid of forever anymore. Maybe she'd been saving it for the right person, the right time.

And perhaps she'd found both at last.

CHAPTER TWENTY-SIX

*B*enjamin Walters sat at the head of his small dining table, his coffee growing cold between his palms. Outside, a light drizzle tapped against the window, turning the streetlamp's glow into wavering streaks of gold across the damp pavement. Normally, the sound soothed him; it reminded him of life's steady rhythms—of patience and time.

But patience had become a far more complicated virtue these days.

On the other side of the table, Rochelle cradled her teacup with both hands, gazing into the steam as though it held answers she hadn't yet admitted she wanted. The soft overhead light tinted her skin in warm, honeyed shades, and Benjamin's gaze lingered on the way her deep-blue headscarf framed her face. He loved it when she wore her hair loose and carefree, curls brushing her shoulders—but there was an intimacy in seeing her like this too, at ease, wrapped in the comfort of his home.

He'd always prided himself on knowing when to move and when to hold still, a skill honed over decades of life's ups and downs. But nothing had prepared him for the delicate balancing act of waiting on Rochelle Jefferson to decide when—if—she'd speak her heart aloud.

Every day, she drew closer in the smallest ways: the fleeting touches that lingered on his arm, the open laughter that spilled from her lips, the speculative tilt of her head when she looked at him like he might just be worth the leap. He felt that closeness thrumming between them now, a subtle tension that made the small kitchen space feel intimate and brimming with possibility.

Yet, she hadn't said the words. And the silence where they might have been spoken pressed in on Benjamin more than he liked to admit.

She glanced up, catching him studying her. "You keep looking at me like that," she said wryly, "and I'm gonna think there's something on my face."

Benjamin set his coffee mug down, a smirk ghosting across his lips. "I'll let you know if I find anything."

Rochelle rolled her eyes, but the spark of warmth behind them told him she liked the attention more than she'd ever confess out loud. It was a look she wore more and more often these days—like she was daring herself to relax, to trust, to risk letting someone in again.

He exhaled, forcibly taming the urge to close the distance between them. He wanted to run his hand along hers, feel the shape of her knuckles, the warmth of her palm. He wanted to lean in, press his mouth to that spot on her shoulder where her skin peeked out from her sweater's loose collar, show her in every possible way that he understood what she'd been through —and that he would wait as long as it took.

Instead, he settled for leaning back in his chair, crossing his arms in a move that felt like it was holding him together. "You were thinking about something just now," he said, letting a trace of curiosity creep into his tone.

Her brows dipped. "Oh, so you read minds now?"

Benjamin huffed a quiet laugh. "I don't have to. You've been quiet for a good ten minutes, Ms. Rochelle. And you only go that silent when something's on your mind."

A beat passed. Rochelle shifted in her seat, sliding her thumb over the rim of her teacup in a slow, thoughtful motion. The brief hush stretched, filled by the gentle drumming of rain outside. She looked toward the window, where the streetlamps cast shimmering patterns across the sidewalk.

"It's silly," she murmured.

Benjamin leaned forward, resting his forearms on the table. "Try me," he coaxed, voice gentler than he intended.

Rochelle hesitated, her fingertip tracing a circle on the table's surface. Finally, she drew a breath and let her gaze wander back to his. "I was just thinking about how different my life looks now." She paused as if testing his reaction, but he kept quiet, giving her space. "Before you showed up at my diner that day, I had everything figured out in my head: my retirement routine, my day-to-day schedule. It was all neat and tidy. And then—" she let out a low chuckle, almost wistful "—there you were, asking me about the daily specials like you didn't already plan on coming back the very next day."

His lips curved at that. "I wasn't too obvious, was I?"

She shot him a mock-scathing look that turned soft at the edges. "You weren't slick at all. But you didn't have to be."

Benjamin felt a subtle wave of relief at her admission. A memory flickered: the first time he'd properly looked at her— really looked—her hands steady on the diner counter, her eyes holding a hint of humor and a sliver of vulnerability. Even then, she'd managed to spark something in him he hadn't felt since Ilene.

He cleared his throat, searching for the right words. "I guess you're right," he allowed. "I wanted an excuse to return for your coffee. And your company."

Rochelle's expression softened—almost reluctant, like she was letting slip a piece of her true feelings. "Yeah, well… I never expected any of this. Not again. Not at this point in my life." Her voice was quieter now, as though carefully picking each phrase.

Benjamin's heart gave a slow, tangible thump. She was so close—he could almost feel her next words brushing the air. She might not say them tonight, but every second that ticked by brought them closer to the surface. A small, hopeful flame smoldered in his chest, fighting against the chill of caution that always followed him.

Instead of pressing her, he laid his knuckles gently against the back of her hand, his touch barely more than a brush. It was enough to remind her that he was right here—supporting her, wanting her. Yet also enough to remind him not to rush. Rochelle had been through her share of heartaches, and she needed to give this new trust in him a chance to grow on its own terms.

For a heartbeat, she didn't move, her eyes downcast as her breath caught in a subtle stutter. Then she lifted her gaze, letting her fingers relax. She didn't intertwine them with his, not quite—but she didn't pull away. And that was progress.

He let out a slow breath, willing the tension in his chest to settle. "Some of the best things in life," he said, "are the ones we never see coming."

Rochelle studied him across the table, the silence between them alive with unspoken truths. It struck him again how much he wanted her to realize just how ready he was—how he wasn't some fleeting visitor in her story. He was here to stay, if she'd have him.

She parted her lips, hesitated, then closed them again. In that small pause, a world of possibilities hovered, shimmering in her eyes like a reflection she hadn't fully embraced.

Benjamin's mind flashed on a daydream of what came next: Rochelle in his living room, flipping channels on the old TV while he stirred soup in the kitchen; the two of them side by side under the greenhouse's glass roof, potting a few spring tomatoes; leaning into each other as the sun set over the B&B's veranda. He wanted those everyday moments that knitted two lives together.

She inhaled deeply, then let it out in a breath that seemed to relieve something inside her. Her hand shifted a fraction closer, her skin brushing his. "You might be onto something," she said quietly.

His chest warmed at that. He recognized what she wasn't saying: *I'm coming around. Don't give up.*

He would never dream of it.

Rochelle cleared her throat, adopting a lighter tone. "You planning on finishing that coffee, or are you just gonna let it get stone-cold?"

Benjamin glanced down at the mug he'd neglected for the last quarter of an hour. A grin tugged at the corners of his mouth. "Probably best I grab a fresh cup," he joked, but he made no move to leave the table. The coffee wasn't what mattered.

For a long moment, neither of them spoke. The small lamp above the table hummed with electrical life, and the rain outside slowed to a gentle patter. Rochelle's shoulders seemed to ease, as if all the swirling thoughts in her head had found a rare peace.

When she finally looked up again, the curve of her mouth was tinged with something that looked suspiciously like hope. "You know," she murmured, "I'm thinking tomorrow I might show up at your B&B again. Help you finalize those date packages—or maybe just keep you company."

Benjamin's pulse jumped. It was an invitation, a cautious step forward. "I'd like that," he said, voice low.

She nodded, and though her guarded nature still lingered in her eyes, there was a new readiness shining through. An acceptance that, eventually, the words they both danced around would have their moment in the light.

Benjamin forced himself to stand, gently taking both of their cups to the sink before he said or did something to push Rochelle too far, too fast. Placing the mugs on the counter, he allowed himself a small, private smile at the soft reflection in the window: Rochelle at his table, her chin propped on her hand, a faint smile on her lips.

There was no need to rush. He'd wait as long as it took for Rochelle to offer those final pieces of her heart. He'd done it once in his life, and he could do it again, because she was worth it.

As if sensing his thoughts, Rochelle glanced over at him, a question in her gaze. He returned her look with a slow, steady nod, as if to say, *I'm here. I'm not going anywhere.*

And he truly wasn't. Because when the day came that she was ready to speak her truth aloud, Benjamin intended to meet it with every ounce of patience, devotion, and love he'd been storing up in the quiet corners of his soul.

In that moment—her fingers on the table's edge, his heart thrumming quietly in his chest—the wait felt less like agony and more like a promise waiting to unfold. He could bear it. He could bear it a thousand times over.

Because once Rochelle decided she was ready?

He'd be right there, arms open, heart steady, offering her a future he couldn't wait to build together.

CHAPTER TWENTY-SEVEN

The late spring air drifting through Rochelle's bedroom window smelled faintly of budding wildflowers and cut grass, as if the entire town of Sweetgum were slowly awakening from a winter slumber. A gentle breeze ruffled the curtains, carrying with it the soft strains of the jazz station playing on her stereo. Saxophones and piano keys tangled in a lazy duet, and Rochelle found herself swaying in time to the melody as she studied her reflection in the mirror.

She wore a slim-fitting white dress patterned with delicate blue petals—a piece she had dug out from the back of her closet because, according to Mei, it would "knock Benjamin off his feet." It was a beautiful dress. One she hadn't felt compelled to wear in years. She smoothed the skirt once more, her fingertips brushing across the silky fabric, her heart fluttering with a mixture of nerves and anticipation.

A dinner meeting, she reminded herself. That's all this was. Benjamin had invited her over to talk about the newest phase of the B&B's marketing plan. They had "official" business to finalize. But the thought of standing across from him in this dress sent a small thrill through her. And that thrill spoke louder than any practical explanation of the night's agenda.

"You're smiling to yourself again," Mei teased from where she lounged on the couch, an orange juice in her hand.

Rochelle startled, turning away from the mirror to face her best friend. "Hmm?"

Mei smirked, tilting her chin at Rochelle's reflection. "That dreamy look in your eye. Don't pretend you weren't picturing that man standing right there next to you."

"I am not." Rochelle crossed her arms, but the warmth in her cheeks must have given her away.

"Oh, please," Mei scoffed, setting her glass down. She stood and circled Rochelle, giving the dress a playful tug here and an approving pat there. "Don't kid yourself, girl. I've seen you wear this before, but you never stand that tall in it. Tonight, you're wearing it for someone."

Rolling her eyes, Rochelle let out a soft laugh—though she didn't deny the accusation. She turned to the window again, gaze drifting over the swaying branches outside. The sun was beginning its descent, bathing the world in gentle hues of lilac and gold. The sight made her stomach flip with a sudden awareness: *I almost missed this.*

She'd spent years convincing herself she was content being alone, that her life of quiet independence was all she needed. But in that reflection—of the woman in a white and blue dress, heart drumming with the possibility of something more—she saw the truth. She had spent so long shielding her heart, too afraid to lose something else precious, that she'd nearly locked the door on a future that felt more alive than anything she'd known in years.

"You used to say romance was for the gullible," Mei whispered, a gentle tease in her voice but also a current of sentiment. "I have the distinct memory of you muttering about not wanting to bury another piece of your heart."

Rochelle pressed her lips together. She had said those things in her darkest moments, when grief clung to her like a second skin. *I've already lost enough; I don't need more heartbreak.* But that was before Benjamin, with his steady patience and that quiet grin that melted her defenses one day at a time. Before he'd shown her that maybe, just maybe, love could endure.

She took a breath, brushing a stray curl behind her ear. "I was scared," she admitted softly. "Didn't want to open myself up just to lose it all over again."

Mei's expression gentled. "You were never a coward, Rochelle. You just needed time." She reached out and squeezed Rochelle's shoulders. "I see it in your eyes now. You're ready."

Maybe she was. That realization settled in Rochelle's chest, not as panic, but as a comforting hum—like the last note of a song that had been building for too long. She gave Mei a grateful smile, then checked her watch. "I'd better go. Don't want to keep our dear Mr. Walters waiting."

Mei's laughter followed her out the door. "I doubt that man minds waiting on you, not one bit."

BY THE TIME Rochelle pulled up in front of Benjamin's home, the lavender sky of dusk had melted into deeper purples and blues. Windows around the neighborhood glowed with warm interior lights, and the hush of evening blanketed the street. Rochelle took a moment to smooth her dress and let out a measured breath before stepping onto the porch.

She hesitated, hand raised to knock. For a heartbeat, the house was utterly still, and the old fear rose in her chest—that trembling worry that anything beautiful might be snatched away. But the memory of Benjamin's patient smile banished it. She knocked gently, two taps, then a pause.

He opened the door almost immediately, as though he had been waiting behind it for her signal.

And for a long moment, neither spoke.

Benjamin's gaze traced her from head to toe, lingering as though he couldn't quite believe she stood there, looking the way she did. The faintest parting of his lips told her exactly what he thought: *Wow.*

Heat flared in Rochelle's cheeks, but she mustered a little smirk, slipping past him into the foyer. "What?" she teased. "Never seen a dress before?"

Benjamin's low chuckle resonated through the small entryway. "Not one that makes me forget my own name." He closed the door behind them. "You look… incredible."

That soft compliment made her pulse flutter, but she wouldn't give him the satisfaction of seeing how thoroughly he'd stirred her. "Well, I had to dress the part," she said briskly, "considering this is an official business meeting."

He laughed—warm, intimate. "Official, right. You'll have to give me a second to collect myself, or I won't be good for any meeting at all."

His eyes sparkled with a familiarity that spoke of countless shared jokes and the unsaid confessions that hung between them every time they drew close. Trying to calm the whirl of nerves in her stomach, Rochelle followed him deeper into the house, letting the gentle lamplight guide them into the dining area.

She stopped short at the sight that greeted her: a makeshift presentation station set up near the table. A whiteboard was propped against a chair, crammed with photos, sketches, scribbled notes, and bright sticky tabs. Arrows pointed from snapshots of candlelit dinners to cozy seating areas, finally landing on a simple silhouette of a wedding scene in the B&B's garden. Rochelle's breath caught.

"Ben..." she said, voice catching around the lump suddenly lodged in her throat.

He moved up beside her, hands sliding into his pockets—an old, comfortable gesture. "I wanted you to see the direction I'm thinking of," he explained quietly. "We've talked about expansions—date packages, romantic weekends—but I realized... we could do so much more."

Rochelle's gaze lingered on the wedding sketch. It was modest—a pair of faceless figures beneath an archway, drawn with shaky lines—yet the meaning behind it slammed into her chest. For an instant, she imagined herself and Benjamin in that spot, exchanging vows surrounded by the sweet smell of his greenhouse blooms and the hush of a late spring day.

She looked up, catching him watching her. His expression was patient—vulnerable, even. He waited, as he always did, letting her process her emotions at her own pace.

Instead of voicing the turbulent swirl of thoughts in her head—*I want to stand under that arch with you. I can't imagine a future without you*—she simply cleared her throat. "You've really outdone yourself," she managed.

"It's just a rough concept," he said, though the pride in his eyes told her it was anything but a passing idea.

She nudged him gently. "Are you sure this is all business, Mr. Walters?"

A lopsided grin curved his lips. "That depends on what you say next, Ms. Rochelle."

They stood there, the hush of the room pressing in. The overhead light cast a golden halo around them, making her acutely aware of how close they were. Her heart picked up a restless beat.

In that breath of silence, Rochelle felt the urge to reveal every last piece of herself—to whisper, *I want you. I want forever.* But the words tangled on her tongue, still heavy with the memory of past heartaches.

She reached out instead, brushing her fingers over the simple wedding silhouette drawn on the board. She didn't miss how his gaze followed her hand, the slightest flicker of hope dancing behind his eyes.

"So," she said softly, forcing a playful note into her voice. "Tell me more about this 'wedding package' you've envisioned."

The corners of Benjamin's mouth quirked upward. "If we offer it, we have to test it out first."

A spark of mischief lit Rochelle's gaze. "And who'd volunteer for that?"

Benjamin shrugged, faux-casual. "Malachi and Aimee might be game."

She let out a low laugh, amused by the faint twitch in his jaw that suggested he was testing her. "Or maybe us," she murmured, allowing the possibility to linger in the air.

He froze.

She felt it like a tangible shift—his steady composure wavering. A quick glance at his face showed the beginnings of astonishment, tempered by the hush of profound relief. She'd said it out loud, no more dancing around the edges. *Maybe us.*

Her heart thudded so hard she wondered if he could hear it. But she forced herself to meet his gaze, letting him read all the sincerity there. She saw his breath catch, a slow inhalation like a diver surfacing after being underwater for too long.

"Rochelle..." he breathed.

There was a wealth of emotion in that one syllable of her name, enough to make her exhale shakily. She didn't back down, not this time. "I don't mean a pretend ceremony," she clarified, voice hushed but resolute. "I mean us, Benjamin. For real."

A raw sound escaped him—something that was half laugh, half sigh of disbelief. He lifted a hand to rub at his jaw, and she watched that moment of vulnerability flicker across his features once more. His eyes darkened with something close to reverence as he reached for her, his palms coming to rest against her cheeks.

Her breath caught at the tenderness in his touch, the way his thumbs skimmed her cheekbones. "You mean that?" he asked, voice trembling just a note.

Rochelle placed her hands over his, letting her eyes flutter shut for a moment. "I do."

He chuckled, the sound thick with joy. "You might want to choose your words carefully," he murmured, "because if you say *I do*, I might just take it literally."

Her laugh danced between them, warm and free. "Maybe that's exactly what I want."

Their lips met—gently at first, a meeting of shared breath and long-awaited yeses that had hovered unspoken for too long. Rochelle's knees threatened to buckle at the flood of emotion rising inside her. This wasn't a tentative step; it was a leap—off the cliffs of fear and regret, into the arms of a man who had been her safe place all along.

Benjamin deepened the kiss, one hand sliding to the nape of her neck, the other still cradling her cheek with a gentleness that nearly undid her. She pressed closer, reveling in the solid warmth of him, the faint spice of his cologne mingling with the promise that hovered in the air. When they pulled away, both were breathless, hearts galloping in unison.

He leaned his forehead against hers, eyes glowing with a happiness she'd never seen him wear so openly. "You just made me the luckiest man alive," he whispered, voice low and weighted with truth.

Emotion thickened Rochelle's throat, but she forced a teasing smile. "I'd better get used to hearing that."

His chest rumbled with quiet laughter. "You're right about that."

He seemed reluctant to let her go, his arms still looped around her waist. She didn't mind. She could get used to standing in this circle of warmth, the soft light overhead, the faint smell of coffee lingering in his kitchen. This was a new chapter in her life—one she had spent decades denying she'd ever read, let alone write herself.

At last, she slid her hands to rest against his chest, feeling the steady thud of his heart. "So," she teased, "do we do the whole traditional proposal thing, or are we skipping straight to me picking out a dress?"

A grin tugged at Benjamin's lips, mischievous and strangely boyish. "Well, you deserve the best. Which means a proper proposal in front of… this." He gestured, quite solemnly, to the aged oven near the back of the kitchen—the one Rochelle knew had broken down on him months ago and eventually led him to her diner.

She let out a whoop of laughter, head tilting back in disbelief. "Your oven, Ben? *Really?* That's where you want to do it?"

He pressed a hand to his heart in mock offense. "That oven is a historic relic in our love story. Without it conking out, I might've never met you."

Shaking her head, Rochelle couldn't hold back a grin. "Well then. Let's do it right."

To her mingled shock and delight, Benjamin dropped to one knee, still wearing that lopsided grin that said this moment was every bit as real as the love blossoming in her chest. He gathered both of her hands in his, gazing up at her with unwavering devotion.

"Rochelle," he began, voice warm and trembling at the same time, "would you make me the happiest man in Sweetgum—and beyond—and marry me?"

The weight of it all—his sincerity, the months of gentle courtship, the years she'd spent convincing herself she'd never trust another man with her heart—surged within her. Her eyes prickled with unshed tears, a laughter-laced sob catching in her throat.

Still, her answer was certain. "Yes, Benjamin Walters," she said, voice trembling with emotion. "I will marry you."

His joy exploded in a bright, unguarded laugh as he rose to sweep her into his arms, spinning her in a circle. The entire world blurred around them—just a swirl of color and light. When he set her down, he sealed the promise with another kiss, slow and reverent. Rochelle's arms wrapped around his shoulders, fingers brushing the nape of his neck. And in that kiss, she felt it all: the new beginning, the redemption of her hope, the future she'd once believed was gone.

When they finally drew apart, her cheeks felt hot, her heart soared, and her soul breathed for the first time in what felt like forever. She pressed her forehead to his, eyes fluttering shut.

"I'm done waiting," she said softly, meaning every syllable.

Benjamin smiled against her cheek, that same steady patience shining in his voice. "So am I."

Rochelle exhaled, letting the contentment wash over her. Letting it anchor her to this place, this man, this moment that would stand as a reminder that sometimes, the leaps in life were the only way to truly land where you belonged.

At last, she had everything she'd feared wanting—and she found herself ready, more than she'd ever been, to embrace it.

CHAPTER TWENTY-EIGHT

Benjamin adjusted the bow tie at his collar with practiced, sure movements, although a ripple of anticipation quivered through him. He eyed himself in the mirror of his bedroom—an older man in a crisp suit with salt-and-pepper hair, posture straight, shoulders squared. The confidence in his reflection wasn't new; he'd worn suits on countless occasions, attended formal gatherings, hosted events. But this was different. Behind the steadiness of his gaze lived something he'd almost forgotten how to recognize:

Hope.

He drew in a slow breath, letting its warmth settle in his chest. He was getting married today—remarrying, even—and the gravity of it pulsed through every breath he took. It was at once exhilarating and humbling. His mind slid backward, unbidden, to memories of another wedding day, decades past. That morning, Ilene had flitted around the room, fussing over the collar of his dress shirt, scolding him for fiddling with his tie. He could still hear her laughter echo in the corners of his memory, still picture the way the sunlight caught the pearls at her neck.

Now, he stood alone. Or rather, not alone—he felt Ilene's presence, not as a weight but as a gentle nudge, urging him forward. His gaze flicked to the bed behind him, the same one he once dreaded looking at after Ilene passed, afraid to stir even a single memory. Over the years, it had become a silent reminder of what he'd lost. Yet today, it felt no heavier than any other piece of furniture—a bed, a place to rest. No longer a shrine to grief, no longer a ghost haunting his quiet moments.

He straightened his cuffs, a small, knowing smile touching his lips. *Rochelle.* The name thrummed through his mind like a steady heartbeat. In the weeks since their engagement, he'd often found himself marveling at how naturally she had slipped into his world. Her vibrancy, her humor, her compassion—they had revived a part of his soul he thought might remain forever dormant.

He knew she'd been afraid. She'd even told him about the terror that tugged at her, the fear of letting someone in again, only to endure the pain of loss. But she had chosen him anyway—chosen them—and he'd waited as long as she needed to stand at this threshold of commitment with confidence. Today they would promise themselves to each other—two souls who had lived enough life to understand what love could cost, and also what it could mean to find it again.

A soft knock broke his reverie.

"Mr. Walters? All the guests are here. Are you ready?" Malachi's voice filtered through the door, muffled but earnest.

Benjamin cast one more glance at the suit in the mirror, patting his jacket pocket to confirm that the vows he'd scribbled down were still there. He picked up the bottle of cologne on the dresser, gave himself a discreet spritz—nothing overpowering, just a subtle note that might reach Rochelle when she leaned in—and then crossed the room. Opening the door, he found Malachi standing in the hallway, dressed in a sharp suit with a silver vest that gleamed under the warm overhead lighting.

"Why yes, I am," Benjamin replied, keeping his voice calm even though excitement soared in his chest.

Malachi stepped inside, closing the door carefully. He scanned the bedroom with a quiet sort of curiosity, as though he was seeing it for the first time. Faint chatter and sporadic bursts of laughter floated through the open window, telling them both that the garden below was filling up with loved ones and friends. The wedding was set to take place among the flowering arches and softly lit paths—an intimate ceremony that Rochelle had once insisted would never happen, yet here they were.

Benjamin moved to the window, letting his gaze drift to the rows of white chairs arranged on the manicured lawn. At the far end stood a simple arbor decorated with pastel blooms— Rochelle's doing, no doubt, if the elegant flourish of ribbons was any indication.

"You okay?" he asked, noticing Malachi's subdued expression as the younger man joined him by the window.

Malachi tucked his hands into his pockets, his posture just a bit rigid. "Yeah... I just—" He paused, a half-laugh escaping him. "It's surreal, you know? Seeing my aunt finally take this step. She's wanted love for so long but convinced herself she didn't. Now here she is, about to marry the man who changed her mind."

Benjamin felt a rush of affection for this nephew who knew Rochelle so intimately, who understood just how many barriers she'd had around her heart. The raw gratitude swelling in his chest made him want to hug the kid. "I'm honored to be that man," he said simply.

Glancing over his shoulder, Malachi nodded. "She's going to say her vows surrounded by the people she helped unite—like Alex and Maia, and all the other couples. It seems fitting, doesn't it? That after years of guiding others toward their own happily ever after, she's finally ready to claim her own."

For a moment, Benjamin's throat tightened. He reached out,

resting a hand on Malachi's shoulder. "Couldn't agree more. She's earned it."

Malachi's face softened, and his gaze flicked from the garden to Benjamin's jacket. "Congratulations to you, too, sir. I heard the B&B's new engagement package is already drawing attention." A smile crept across his lips. "People are sold on the idea of finding love in a place that gave you and Aunt Rochelle a second chance. Word's spread like wildfire."

Benjamin chuckled, pride mixing with a warm sense of humility. "I can't take too much credit. Rochelle's behind a lot of the creativity… and her story resonates with people."

"She's the talk of Sweetgum," Malachi agreed. "They're calling it the perfect next chapter for the diner queen who never thought she'd wear a wedding dress again."

"She does capture an audience," Benjamin said, a smile tugging at his mouth. He pictured Rochelle at the diner in her prime—confidence radiating as she took orders, teased customers, and doled out sage advice like it was second nature. It still amazed him that the same woman who exuded that fearless energy had also harbored such deep uncertainties about her own future. And yet, here she was, about to transform the B&B's garden into a place of vows and renewed faith in love.

Malachi cleared his throat, brightening. "You're in for a treat, sir. Aimee and the ladies spent hours fussing over every detail of Rochelle's look. I glimpsed them setting up in one of the B&B rooms, but I got ushered away. All I know is she'll have you speechless. Then again," he added with a grin, "she could wear a potato sack, and you'd still think she's the most stunning woman in the world, right?"

Benjamin snorted a laugh, his heart thrumming. "She already is," he confirmed, each word laden with sincerity.

A flicker of fondness passed across Malachi's features, and he patted Benjamin's arm. "Well, I think we've kept her waiting long enough."

Benjamin nodded, turning away from the window. Nervous excitement simmered beneath his composure, a type of anticipation he hadn't felt in decades. He pictured Rochelle in her dress—whatever style she'd chosen—and the moment when their eyes would lock, the entire crowd falling away into a soft blur of color and light. He let out a steadying breath, reminding himself to take it all in, to be fully present for every step of this experience.

He followed Malachi out into the corridor, running a final mental checklist: The officiant was already outside, the rings were safe in the best man's pocket (Mei had teased that *she* wanted to hold them, but tradition won out), and the guests—all the beloved friends, including those Rochelle had matched over the years—were in their seats. Most importantly, his vows were tucked in his jacket, ready to be spoken from the heart.

As he reached the stairs, the quiet hush of the house broke into a cascade of cheerful voices drifting from below, and he felt a swirl of butterflies dance in his stomach. It occurred to him how incredible it was to be standing at this threshold again— older, yes, and maybe wiser, but still brimming with the hopeful eagerness of a groom on his wedding day.

"She's waiting for you," Malachi murmured, voice low but encouraging.

Benjamin's fingers brushed against the polished banister. He glanced at the young man who'd become so important to Rochelle, so important to him, too. "Thank you," he said softly. "For everything. For supporting her, for supporting us."

Malachi nodded, stepping aside with a gentle smile. "I wouldn't miss this for the world."

And with that, Benjamin descended the stairs, heading toward the back doors where the garden awaited. Each step seemed to echo with memories of Ilene's bright laughter, of Rochelle's hesitant but determined smiles, of every moment that had led him here. Yet, the weight of the past did not hinder him;

it bolstered him, reminding him how precious and fleeting this second chance was.

Stepping outside, the evening air embraced him—mild, scented with roses and fresh-cut grass. Rows of guests turned their heads, smiling and murmuring their approval. He caught glimpses of familiar faces: Stan from the diner, a newly-engaged couple who'd just booked a stay at the B&B, longtime friends who'd known him since before he was ever a bed-and-breakfast owner. They all looked at him with warmth and joy, but Benjamin's gaze slid past them, searching for one face in particular.

He found her, waiting just inside a small canopy near the edge of the lawn, her figure shielded by the shadows. A shape in white—the details hidden from his vantage point, but he felt the magnetic pull of her presence all the same. In that moment, nerves and excitement blended into one potent wave, making his heart slam against his ribcage.

This is really happening, he thought, inhaling to steady himself. He smiled, and it was the kind of smile that reached his eyes, that smoothed the years from his face, that made him remember why he had waited. Because for Rochelle, waiting had always been worth it. Every second of patience, every quiet reassurance, every slow step forward—they had all led to this single day, this single promise.

He settled at his spot beneath the floral arch, turning to face the guests, hands clasped loosely in front of him. A hush settled over the garden, expectant and brimming with joy. Benjamin let his shoulders relax, the tension in his body giving way to gratitude. His eyes flicked to Malachi, who gave him a subtle nod from the side, looking half-proud, half-tearful.

A faint wisp of music drifted through the air, the first chords of the song Rochelle had chosen to walk down the aisle. The hush deepened; even the birds seemed to hold their breath. And in that charged silence, Benjamin felt the fullness of this moment surge through him like a warm tide.

He thought about Ilene—how she'd taught him to cherish every sunrise. She'd have been the first to insist he find happiness again. *And here I am, Ilene,* he murmured inwardly. *I found it. I found her.*

His pulse quickened. Rochelle stepped out from beneath the canopy, and for the space of a heartbeat, the world stopped turning. The details of her dress, the subtle glow of her makeup, the steady determination in her eyes—it took his breath away. She was radiant in every sense of the word, carrying herself with the poise of a woman who had finally chosen to embrace love without fear.

Benjamin's heart soared, and an unspoken vow bloomed in his chest: *I will love her, guard her hopes, respect her fears, and celebrate her triumphs.* He'd do whatever was necessary to keep that luminous look of joy on her face.

She met his gaze, her lips curving into a soft, uncertain smile —uncertain not because she doubted, but because the enormity of it all was as overwhelming for her as it was for him. And in that look, he read every silent promise, every leap of faith that had carried them to this moment.

Benjamin could barely contain the rush of emotions threatening to tighten his throat. As Rochelle came closer, step by step, he felt his soul settle into a calm certainty: This was it—the life he wanted to forge, side by side with her, day after day, for the rest of their years.

And as she finally stopped in front of him, her hands trembling slightly in his, he realized he hadn't just waited for her— he'd been waiting for this fullness of life. For the last puzzle piece to click into place, proving that second chances weren't just fanciful stories—they could be real, vibrant, and entirely worth the waiting.

He squeezed her fingers, unable to stop the grin that split his face. And when she squeezed back, the entire garden seemed to exhale in quiet wonder, as though everyone there understood: This was a promise a long time in the making, one that was every bit as powerful now as it had been the first time Benjamin Walters ever stood at a wedding altar.

And in his heart, he thought: *At last.*

CHAPTER TWENTY-NINE

Rochelle barely recognized the woman staring back at her from the oval mirror. The carefully pinned hair, the delicate lace gliding over her curves—all of it felt both foreign and deeply, achingly right. She lifted trembling fingers to the bodice of her wedding dress, smoothing down a minuscule wrinkle in the soft ivory fabric. It was simple, timeless, just as she'd wanted—enough to honor the depth of this day without all the unnecessary frills.

Behind her, Aimee and Mrs. Zhang fluttered with nervous excitement, while Mrs. Bridges double-checked Rochelle's veil. A small part of Rochelle still marveled that she was wearing a veil at all, but the others had insisted.

"You need a hint of drama," Aimee had teased.

"This moment deserves every ounce of beauty," Mrs. Bridges had agreed as she fastened the delicate tulle in place.

Now, Rochelle glanced at herself and felt the corners of her lips lift in a smile—tremulous but genuine. *A bride.* She had been so many things in her life: caregiver to Malachi, owner of a bustling diner, reluctant retiree, matchmaker to half the couples in Sweetgum. Yet here she was, in a role she had never truly expected to claim again.

She inhaled deeply, pressing both hands to her abdomen in a vain attempt to calm the butterflies dancing inside. Outside, she could hear the faint hum of guests chatting, distant strums of a violin—and, closer still, the soft shuffle of people moving about in the corridors of the B&B. It was all so real, so immediate.

"Alright, now," Mrs. Bridges said, stepping back and studying Rochelle from head to toe. "You're ready."

Ready.

The word caught in Rochelle's throat, sending a thrill through her. Two months ago, if someone had predicted she'd be stepping into a white dress, preparing to walk down an aisle toward a man who had waited so patiently for her, she'd have laughed in their face. She would've pointed to her age, her scars, her pragmatic outlook, and declared herself past such romantic notions.

But that was before Benjamin.

Aimee and Mrs. Zhang hovered by the door, exchanging mischievous smiles. In their eyes, Rochelle saw unwavering support—and a flicker of triumph, as though both women had always known this was where she belonged.

Rochelle let out a wobbly laugh, placing a hand over her heart. Her pulse throbbed beneath her fingertips, not in fear, but in *excitement, longing, love.*

She looked down at her dress. The lace felt like a promise: delicate yet surprisingly strong. In some ways, it reminded her of the walls she'd spent years constructing—intricate, layered, but capable of tearing if pulled the wrong way. Benjamin had never yanked or forced; he'd simply waited for her to open up each layer at her own pace.

The realization hit her again: *She wanted him. Now, tomorrow, forever.* He was no fleeting romance. He was the anchor she hadn't realized she'd been missing.

Emotion swelled in her chest, so bright and fierce that she had to grip the vanity's edge to steady herself. She blinked, and a tear escaped—a tear of disbelief and joy and a thousand other things she couldn't name.

"Something funny, dear?" Mrs. Zhang asked, arching a brow.

Rochelle shook her head, eyes shining. "I've just… never been more certain of anything in my life."

Aimee's eyes welled with tears as she rushed forward, mindful not to wrinkle the dress as she hugged Rochelle. "I'm so happy for you," she whispered, voice trembling with emotion.

Mrs. Zhang patted Rochelle's shoulder gently. "We've all been waiting for you to take this leap. Benjamin was always ready, but we needed you to see it too."

Rochelle laughed softly, stepping out of their embrace. "I suppose I made everyone wait a bit too long, huh?"

There was a light knock at the door just then, and Mrs. Bridges poked her head in. "They're ready for you in the garden, honey."

Ready.

Rochelle swallowed, the word echoing in her mind once more. With trembling fingers, she smoothed the gown one last time, gave her reflection a final glance, and straightened her shoulders. "Let's do this."

SHE FOLLOWED MRS. BRIDGES, Mrs. Zhang, and Aimee into the hallway, the faint strains of violins growing clearer with each step they took toward the garden exit. A hush of anticipation seemed to shiver in the air. It reminded Rochelle of the quiet before dawn—filled with the promise of a new day.

Malachi waited just outside the threshold, impeccably dressed and looking more grown-up than she ever remembered. Her heart pinched at the memory of him as a child—so full of questions, so trusting, always making her laugh. She had watched him become the man he was now. In many ways, he'd been the reason she'd set aside romance and devoted herself to giving him the best possible life.

Now, he offered his arm to her, his smile a bit too proud. "Auntie, I…" He trailed off, eyes brimming with admiration. "You look beautiful. More than that—happy."

Rochelle linked her arm with his, giving it a comforting squeeze. "That's exactly how I feel."

They stepped outside, onto a winding stone path that led toward the heart of the B&B's garden. A small canopy stretched overhead—a last bit of cover shielding her from the audience's view for just a moment longer. Soft chatter and whispers reached her ears from beyond the canopy's edge, and her pulse thundered in time with each gentle violin note wafting on the spring breeze.

This is real, she thought, cheeks warming. She was about to walk toward a man who had steadfastly guarded her heart even before she'd admitted it was his to keep.

Malachi led her to the edge of the canopy. A hush seemed to fall over the guests, and Rochelle felt the collective anticipation gathering in the air. Then the violinists shifted into a new tune, light and lilting, a melody that wove directly into Rochelle's heart.

She drew a breath, and there, through the arch of chairs and the faint shimmer of fresh blossoms, stood Benjamin.

Nothing could have prepared her for the look on his face. She'd seen him in quiet moments, in laughter, in soft vulnerability—but never quite like this. His gaze locked on her as though she were the only person in the world. The gentlest curve of his lips told her more than words ever could: *He was ready for forever, and he had no doubt that she was worth every second of waiting.*

Tears threatened, but Rochelle blinked them back, determined to keep this moment clear and bright. With each slow, measured step, she felt the tension of the past—her fears, her hesitations—unravel. In their place bloomed wonder, confidence, and an overwhelming gratitude that life had given her this second chance.

The aisle seemed both endless and far too short. She caught sight of familiar faces—friends she'd matched, neighbors who'd watched her grow from a busy diner owner to a reluctant retiree, now turned soon-to-be bride. Their expressions shimmered with collective joy.

All the while, her gaze kept returning to Benjamin. He stood beneath a floral arbor, the slight breeze ruffling his salt-and-pepper hair, his eyes shining with unshed tears. The suit he wore highlighted his broad shoulders, but it was the warmth in his expression that stole Rochelle's breath.

His silent, reverent stare wrapped around her like the gentlest embrace, promising that no matter what came next, they would face it together—comfort and patience, passion and laughter, woven through each day to come.

Finally, she reached him, the scent of roses mingling with the sweet crispness of spring. Malachi released her arm gently, stepping aside with a look that said he couldn't be prouder. Rochelle lifted her gaze to Benjamin, who was close enough now for her to see the faint lines of relief and happiness crinkling at the corners of his eyes.

She let out a shaky exhale, and he took her hands in his, steadying them against the tremor she couldn't quite suppress. His touch was everything familiar—warm, reassuring, a safe haven she had once believed she'd never find again.

For a moment, they simply stood there, hearts beating in tandem. A hush fell across the garden, the violin's melody softening to a gentle undercurrent, and Rochelle felt the weight of each precious heartbeat.

Benjamin's lips parted, and in that single glance, she felt the unspoken vow: *I will love you, protect you, nurture every hope you've dared to hold.*

She drew in a breath, her own vow stirring deep in her chest: *I choose you, Benjamin Walters. Today, tomorrow, always.*

She might have spoken it aloud had the officiant not cleared his throat discreetly, preparing to begin the ceremony. Yet those words stayed perched on her lips, ready to be released when the time came.

As she and Benjamin turned together to face the small crowd —everyone from Mrs. Zhang to Aimee and Malachi, from old diner regulars to newly engaged couples who'd heard about Sweetgum's "matchmaker bride"—Rochelle couldn't stop the smile trembling at the edges of her mouth. She had spent her life helping others find love, never imagining that love would circle back and embrace her in such a grand, unexpected way.

Now she stood here, dressed in lace and carrying the fullness of her heart, walking toward forever with the man who had waited without question, without demand—just unwavering faith that she'd one day see what he saw. And she had.

As the officiant's voice rose softly over the hush, Rochelle squeezed Benjamin's hand. He squeezed back, a tender spark passing between them. The past slipped away like an old chapter carefully concluded, and a brand-new story stretched out before them.

She let that last wall within her crumble, letting in every ounce of joy, every note of the violins, every murmured blessing from the gathering. *This is where I belong,* she thought, raising her eyes once more to Benjamin's, which shimmered with devotion.

I am ready. At last.

CHAPTER THIRTY

The violinists' notes shifted like a breeze catching newly unfurled petals, soft and fluttering. Benjamin drew in a quiet breath, letting the music guide him to a place of stillness. He wasn't nervous. That part surprised him a little—people always said a groom's heart pounded with anxiety at the altar. But his wasn't pounding in fear or worry. It was pounding with awe.

He stood beneath a simple arch woven with pale blooms and trailing ribbons, the spring sunlight gilding the garden. Rows of guests turned expectant eyes his way, then toward the path leading from the B&B. He glanced around briefly—spots of color from well-worn dresses, the hush of small conversations tapering off, the wisp of violin melody threading the air. And then, like a slow wave, the crowd fell silent.

The soft rustle of fabric signaled her arrival. He looked up, and everything else ceased to exist.

Rochelle stepped from behind the small canopy at the far corner of the garden. The way the sun hit the gossamer veil at her shoulders created a halo-like glow, and Benjamin's breath caught in his throat. He'd caught a glimpse of her not long ago—

a quick vision under that canopy while he took his own place—but this was different. Now, she stood in full view, grace and courage radiating with every step.

He couldn't begin to focus on the details of her dress—although he saw enough to note how perfectly it skimmed her figure, how delicate lace traced her arms. He barely registered the flowers or veil. It was the look in her eyes that undid him: a luminous certainty, a readiness that made him feel both anchored and weightless all at once.

His fingers twitched at his side, fighting the powerful urge to reach for her now. Not yet, he reminded himself. *Just a moment more. Let her come to you.*

She descended the aisle on Malachi's arm, and the pride in the young man's face was unmistakable. Benjamin sensed something kindred in Malachi's gaze—an understanding of how long Rochelle's heart had been shielded and how monumental this moment was. Malachi looked almost solemn, as though carrying out a sacred duty in escorting the aunt who had raised him toward the man who loved her fiercely enough to wait.

Each step Rochelle took felt like a quiet declaration. She was calm, no trembling, no flicker of doubt behind her bright eyes. This was not a woman who hesitated. This was a woman who had weighed her past fears and chosen love in spite of them. A new, unstoppable warmth spread through Benjamin's chest, stirring tears behind his eyes.

When they finally reached him, Malachi paused. He turned to Rochelle, holding her hands for a tender second. "You look beautiful, Auntie," he whispered, and Rochelle's lips trembled in a grateful smile.

Malachi then faced Benjamin, jaw set with gentle resolve. "You take care of her," he said, quietly but firmly, echoing a vow that needed no real response.

Benjamin inclined his head without hesitation. "Always," he promised, his tone unwavering.

Satisfied, Malachi stepped aside, letting Rochelle move the last step alone. She placed her hand in Benjamin's outstretched one, and the instant her fingers pressed into his palm, Benjamin felt something slot into place—as though the entire universe clicked into perfect alignment.

He breathed in the faint scent of her perfume, closed his eyes for a beat, and let awe flood him. *We're here. We really made it.*

The ceremony itself felt like a dream unfolding in slow motion. The minister's voice rose gently, guiding them through the formalities, while the spring breeze ruffled the ribbons overhead. Birds trilled faintly at the edge of the garden, a sweet natural harmony to the violin playing nearby. Rochelle's veil fluttered, catching the light and turning every breath of air into a shimmer around her hair.

When it came time for the vows, Benjamin inhaled deeply, gathering every bit of gratitude in his chest. He held both her hands in his, focusing on the warmth of her skin against his. Looking into her eyes, he began:

"Rochelle," he said, voice tinged with emotion he didn't bother to hide, "from the day I first stepped into your diner, you made me feel at home. You welcomed me, a stranger, without questioning who I was or why I kept coming back. And in doing so, you gave me something I never expected to find again: a sense of belonging. Of possibility." He paused, a gentle smile curving his lips. "I thought I was too old to love again, that my time had passed. But you showed me that love isn't limited by age or circumstance. It's a gift we can accept any time we're brave enough to open our hearts."

He felt Rochelle's fingertips tremble slightly, and it gave him the courage to push on. "I promise," he continued softly, "to hold your hand when the days are hard, to celebrate with you when the days are sweet, and to stand by you through every sunrise and sunset we're blessed to share. I'd wait a thousand lifetimes if I had to, Rochelle, if it meant getting the chance to love you in each one."

A collective sigh whispered through the crowd. Benjamin noticed wetness at the corners of Rochelle's eyes as she pressed her lips together, half-laughing, half-tearing up. He nearly lost his composure right there, but a steady breath pulled him back to the moment.

Then it was her turn. She gathered herself, blinking to clear her tears. Her gaze found his, and the love in her eyes was fierce and tender all at once.

"Benjamin," she said, voice husky with emotion, "I spent years telling myself that love was something I'd already tasted once, something I lost, and that I wasn't meant to have it again. I built a safe life—lonely at times, sure—but safe. I told myself I didn't need anyone. Didn't need a warm hand to hold or a gentle voice to remind me that I deserved happiness too."

Her lips trembled, and she squeezed his hands, a tear trailing down her cheek. "But then, you walked in like it was the most natural thing in the world, making my diner feel like home for you and me both. You showed me patience when I didn't even realize how badly I needed it. You stood by, quietly and faithfully, while I sorted through my own hesitations. You never pushed, never rushed. And through your kindness, your laughter, your calm presence, I learned something I was too scared to believe: that my heart could open up again." She paused, exhaling a shaky laugh. "So I promise to walk beside you, no matter what life throws at us. I promise to let you in, even when old fears try to sneak back. And above all, I promise to love you for as many days as we have—no matter how many that might be."

Somewhere in the crowd, someone sniffled audibly. Rochelle reached up, lightly brushing a tear from Benjamin's cheek. He hadn't even realized he was crying. Heat filled his face, but he welcomed it, letting the surge of love wash through him.

The minister's voice broke the hush that followed, pronouncing them husband and wife in words that seemed both surreal and unquestionably true. "You may now kiss the bride," he said, and Benjamin didn't need to be told twice.

He drew Rochelle close, one hand cupping the back of her neck, the other sliding around her waist. She fit against him like a missing piece, and the moment their lips met, the weight of forever settled in his chest with sweet inevitability. There was a roar of applause and cheers, but he barely heard it—his entire universe narrowed to the softness of Rochelle's mouth, the quiet sigh that left her lips, the hum of joy in his veins.

They broke apart to find the guests on their feet—Mei wiping away tears, Aimee and Malachi wearing matching grins, Stan from the diner clapping so hard his shoulders shook. Rochelle pressed her forehead to Benjamin's, laughing a little breathlessly.

"Took me long enough to get here, huh?" she teased, voice quavering with all the emotion brimming inside.

Benjamin brushed his thumb against her cheek, his heart pounding in time with the thunderous applause around them. "I'd have waited as long as it took," he murmured back, low enough for only her to hear. "And I'd do it all again."

A watery laugh shook her shoulders, and she wound her arms around his neck. "Well, now I'm not going anywhere," she promised, a playful twinkle in her eye. "So I hope you're ready to live with me hogging all the blankets and complaining about your morning coffee routine."

He chuckled, pressing a light kiss to her temple. "Darlin', you can hog every blanket we own. As long as I wake up next to you, I'll never complain."

She beamed, and for a moment, the crowd's cheering seemed to fade behind the warmth of her smile. This was their moment —one forged in patience and fear and hope. One that confirmed they were bound by more than vows; they were bound by understanding, by a promise that love could indeed come again, unexpectedly and beautifully, even after heartache.

The minister raised his hands to invite everyone to join in the celebration, and the violins kicked into a livelier tune. Rochelle leaned in, close enough for Benjamin to see the sparkle in her eyes. "So, Mr. Walters," she asked, arching a brow in mock challenge, "are you ready for all that forever business you kept talking about?"

He grinned, slipping his hand into hers and giving it a gentle, confident squeeze. "Forever starts right now, Mrs. Walters."

And as they turned together, walking back down the aisle to the sound of jubilant applause, he knew beyond a shadow of a doubt that every second spent waiting for this day—every moment of gentle patience, every slow-building spark—had been worth it. Because in Rochelle's laughter and the touch of her hand, he had found something that transcended time, anchored him in hope, and whispered that at long last, they were exactly where they were meant to be.

CHAPTER THIRTY-ONE

The diner hummed with laughter and warmth, the low chatter of guests mingling with the soft croon of a classic love song. Tiny string lights—lovingly strung up by Malachi and Aimee—cast a cozy glow across the space, illuminating a night that felt both brand-new and long overdue.

Rochelle sat at the counter, the same old swivel stool she'd occupied a hundred times before. But this time was different—so different. Because now, her world had quietly, irrevocably shifted. She lifted her gaze to the man beside her, his hand covering hers in a gentle, steady grip.

Benjamin.

Her husband.

His thumb traced slow circles against her palm, as though the rest of the diner and all its boisterous energy didn't exist. The weight of that small gesture wrapped itself around Rochelle's heart. She felt him in every soft press of his thumb, every brush of his skin against hers—felt the certainty behind it, the promise that they were in this for keeps.

"Fresh from the oven! Come and get 'em!"

Aimee's bright voice rang out from behind the counter,

proudly presenting a tray of steaming pastries. Rochelle smelled melted cheese and toasted dough, recognized the delicious swirl of comfort food meant to keep the evening relaxed and light. It teased up old memories—late-night snacks at the diner, quick bites shared over jokes and whispered confessions.

She glanced around, taking in the sight of friends and neighbors gathered in celebration. Clusters of people laughed and reminisced; Mrs. Zhang chatted animatedly with one of Benjamin's groomsmen, her hands moving in lively arcs. Over by the jukebox, Brandi and Chris gently swayed in a slow dance, lost in their own moment. And in a quiet corner, Malachi stood with Aimee, sharing a private joke that made her giggle behind her champagne flute.

For a second, Rochelle's throat tightened with affection. She wondered if there might be another wedding to plan soon—Aunt Rochelle never turned off her matchmaking radar, after all. She reached for her coffee mug, only to find it empty, and turned just in time to see Benjamin setting down his own drink.

"Feeling overwhelmed yet?" she teased, nudging him lightly with her elbow.

His responding smile was soft, his gaze lingering on the room. "Not overwhelmed," he murmured. "Just... taking it all in."

She followed the path of his eyes—saw the look of quiet contentment, the way his shoulders seemed relaxed and at home. *Our people*, she thought, eyes sweeping over the lively crowd, the diner's neon sign gleaming just outside the windows. *Our life*.

"Congrats again, you two," came a friendly voice. Brandi sidled up with a small plate of food. "I don't think I've ever seen the diner sparkle quite like this."

Rochelle snorted, waving off the compliment. "Oh, hush. It's just the same old place—plus a few string lights."

Brandi cocked an eyebrow. "And a whole lot of love," she

said with a wink, dropping her voice conspiratorially. "You should see how that man looks at you. He's already planning how to sneak you away for some private newlywed time."

Heat rushed to Rochelle's cheeks. The grin Benjamin flashed from over Brandi's shoulder told her he'd heard every word.

She turned, arching a brow. "Something funny, Mr. Walters?"

He shook his head, smirking. "Nothing at all, Mrs. Walters."

Mrs. Walters.

She'd heard it in the ceremony, of course—but hearing it now, in the midst of their friends, at the diner she'd poured so much of her heart into, made it feel infinitely more real. Her chest tightened, not from fear this time, but from the breathtaking knowledge that she had chosen this—chosen him, chosen them.

Brandi offered a quick, knowing smile before melting back into the crowd, and Rochelle shifted her focus to Benjamin. She wanted to say something witty, to keep up the banter that had always flowed so easily between them. But before she could form the words, the music shifted, a gentle piano melody drifting through the air.

She recognized the song instantly—*their* song.

Benjamin's fingers brushed deliberately against hers, an unspoken invitation. Rochelle let out a short, playful sigh and let him lead her away from the counter, toward the small patch of linoleum cleared for dancing. Conversations hushed, guests turning to watch with fond smiles.

He slipped an arm around her waist, tugging her closer, and the simple intimacy of that one motion made her heart pound. She lifted her hand to his shoulder, the other resting comfortably in his warm grasp.

"You did this, didn't you?" she murmured, tilting her head to look into his face.

CHAPTER THIRTY-ONE

A sly grin curved his lips. "I might've whispered a request to Brandi."

Rochelle rolled her eyes, though she couldn't hide the smile tugging at her mouth. "Romantic old fool."

He chuckled, deep and warm, before spinning her gently. The skirt of her simple wedding dress flared around her knees, and Rochelle inhaled a tiny gasp at how effortlessly he guided her. In that moment, there were no onlookers, no diner, no clattering silverware—just the muted sound of their song and the gentle, swaying motion of their dance.

Then he dipped her. Not one of those dramatic, stagey dips, but slow and careful, as though he were giving her time to feel every inch of the moment. Rochelle's breath seized at the back of her throat. She clutched his shoulders, heart thudding so wildly that she wondered if he felt it.

When he drew her back upright, their faces hovered inches apart. She could see the faint crinkles at the edges of his eyes, and the way his gaze darkened with an emotion she wasn't used to seeing so openly in a man's face.

"Say that again?" he teased, voice low.

Her pulse rioted, and for a split second, she could only stare, tongue-tied. Then she found her footing in the only way she knew how—through teasing banter that cloaked just how undone she felt. "You heard me," she managed, trying to steady her voice. "Romantic. Old. Fool."

His nose brushed hers in the lightest, most fleeting of touches. "Only for you," he whispered, and every nerve in Rochelle's body went molten.

It was impossible to ignore the wild leap of her pulse, the tingling wave that rolled up her spine at his words. She had teased him, calling him a fool, but the truth was that he was so far from foolish. He was deliberate, steady, patient—the man who'd waited for her to open her heart after she'd spent years locking it away.

And in that tiny, electrifying moment—noses brushing, the distant hum of conversation fading—she realized he was right: he *was* romantic. Only for her. Only in the ways she hadn't dared hope for again.

The music ended, but she barely heard the last note. He pressed a slow kiss to her temple, the warmth of his lips sending fresh sparks through her veins. Rochelle closed her eyes, letting the hush of the crowd wash over them. For the briefest heartbeat, time felt suspended—her sense of self pinned squarely on the awareness that she was in love.

Really, fully, irrevocably in love.

When she opened her eyes, the applause and soft cheers of their friends came rushing back. Benjamin loosened his hold just enough for them to step back, but his hand lingered, fingertips gliding down her arm before slipping away. Her body ached at the loss, and she exhaled slowly to calm the wild flutter in her chest.

She shot him a look, half-lidded with emotion. "You keep that up, Mr. Walters, and I'll start believing you're out to sweep me right off my feet again."

He laughed, a quiet rumble. "That's exactly the plan, Mrs. Walters."

Mrs. Walters. The words glowed like a brand in her mind, comforting yet thrilling—like everything she'd once thought impossible was now hers to hold. A swirl of mingled fear and exhilaration welled in her chest, and she reached for his hand on instinct, intertwining their fingers.

She didn't want to speak, didn't want to shatter the fragile magic with overthinking. Instead, she let him guide her back toward the counter, where the bustle of the diner carried on around them—familiar yet tinged with the wonder of this new chapter they'd stepped into.

They were still the same Rochelle and Benjamin, with the same banter and teasing, the same small gestures of caring. Yet everything had changed. *She* had changed—from the solitary diner owner who believed her chance at love had passed, to the woman who'd found the courage to claim happiness again.

And as she settled beside him, the glimmer of a ring on her finger catching the light, she felt a quiet, determined promise settle in her chest. This wasn't just about the dance or the wedding day or the ring—it was about every moment after, every sunrise shared, every mundane or extraordinary day they'd face together.

She let out a soft sigh and turned, meeting Benjamin's gaze. The gentle question in his eyes—*You okay?*—brought a swell of warmth to her throat. She squeezed his hand, a faint smile curling her lips.

"I'm fine," she murmured. "Better than fine."

He opened his mouth to speak, but the glint in her eyes seemed to stop him, as if they both recognized that sometimes words weren't enough. There would be plenty of time for more conversation later—long nights of pillow talk, mornings with quiet coffee, days spent planning the future they never thought they'd have.

For now, she leaned in closer, nestling beneath the comforting curve of his shoulder. Outside the diner windows, the evening sky swathed Sweetgum in a deep, star-strewn darkness, and inside these walls was everything she needed: laughter, friends, music…and the man whose touch she never wanted to be without.

This, she thought, her heart full and steady, *is exactly where I'm meant to be.*

Rochelle tore the July page from her kitchen calendar with a decisive snap, her gaze skimming the words scrawled in the margins—reminders of meetings, special dinners, and the everyday routine that had led them here. She let out a small, satisfied hum as she crossed the room, the kettle's sharp whistle filling the air. With a careful hand, she poured steaming water over fresh coffee grounds in her favorite mug, the swirl of rising steam blending with the warm, homey scent of their apartment.

Benjamin sat at the kitchen table, a neat stack of mail in front of him. He paused over an envelope adorned with a stylish magazine logo, squinting a little as he read the return address. "This one looks like it's from a magazine," he said, lifting his eyes to Rochelle just as she came around with the kettle to fill his mug. "Thank you, sweetheart," he murmured, stirring coffee granules that dissolved almost instantly in the hot water.

Rochelle slid into the chair opposite him, blowing on her drink before taking a careful sip. "A magazine?" she repeated. "What's that got to do with us?" She crossed her legs, letting her eyes flick toward the old radio on the counter that crackled with low news chatter. The apartment felt increasingly like home—she'd been here so often before moving in, there wasn't much to adjust to. Still, saying goodbye to her old place had been harder than she'd expected. Four months later, though, the memories felt less like loss and more like a gentle reminder of how far she'd come. Sleeping beside Benjamin each night in the top-floor suite of their budding "romance resort" had more than made up for any lingering nostalgia.

Her husband—she still loved the ring of that word—slid a folded note out of the envelope and skimmed it. "Would you look at that..." he said, handing it across to Rochelle before returning to his breakfast. They each had a plate of eggs, sunny-side up—the kind that Rochelle prided herself on perfecting. She allowed Benjamin in the kitchen sometimes, but he mostly cooked on "special occasions," which always tickled her. He had once made a mean Italian dinner that still gave her goose bumps just thinking about it.

Rochelle straightened, her chest swelling as she read. "So they want to interview us? Find out our secret?" she said with a small laugh. The magazine, called *Simply Sweet*, was a new local feature that had started as a small newspaper column and ballooned into a full publication covering the "happenings" of Sweetgum. With the town rapidly expanding and businesses thriving, it made sense. She still wasn't sure how she felt about the speed of it all—new developments popping up practically overnight—but as long as her business thrived, she couldn't complain too loudly.

Of course, the expansion had drawbacks. Land developers with shiny brochures and big-city accents kept poking around her and Benjamin's resort, waving money in front of them. She and Benjamin had agreed they weren't selling. The proposals came almost weekly, but the answer never changed.

"They don't actually want 'trade secrets,'" Benjamin clarified. "They think our love story would make a great column. There's a note about needing a photo. Maybe we can take a new one—something to keep our wedding picture company in the living room?"

Rochelle's gaze drifted to the framed wedding portrait on their TV stand. In it, she and Benjamin were looking at each other with an unguarded warmth that made her heart skip every time she noticed it. "We did look good that day," she agreed, smiling at the memory. Reliving that event in her dreams every night—and waking up to Benjamin—still felt like the best gift life had given her. "We can give them a call, sure. Maybe tomorrow." She paused to take a bite of her eggs. "But first, who's going to watch the place today? You or me?"

They had expanded their staff well beyond just themselves and Benjamin's old secretary. More housekeepers, more part-time helpers—enough to ensure the "hit romance resort" ran like a well-oiled machine. Rochelle felt a spark of pride each time she walked the halls and saw their guests—couples, fami-lies—enjoying what they'd built. The numbers told her their dream was becoming something sustainable, even if it was happening faster than she'd anticipated.

Benjamin cleared his throat and took a sip of coffee. "I'll watch the resort. You can go catch up with Mei at her restau-rant. Maybe see if that same land developer is still trying to bribe her."

Rochelle rolled her eyes, laughing softly. "You love teasing those men, don't you?" She tested her mug—just the right temperature now—and sipped contentedly. "At least they seem to be getting the message. We haven't seen nearly as many swarming around as before."

Benjamin's expression grew thoughtful. "True. Last week, it felt like they were everywhere—fancy suits, shiny cars from some big city, sniffing around for properties. But this week, we've only spotted one or two. Could be they've realized we're not interested in selling."

She patted his hand. "Don't strain that brilliant mind of yours first thing in the morning. Let's just enjoy our breakfast." She polished off the rest of her coffee and quickened her pace with the eggs. "Gotta eat fast if I'm going to see Mei before the lunch rush. You'll be okay on your own?"

Benjamin's eyes sparkled with good humor. "Of course. Just call me if any more of those suits show up—I'll be sure to give them a piece of my mind." He winked when Rochelle snorted.

IT WAS ONLY ten in the morning, but Mei's restaurant was already packed, every seat full of eager patrons. Rochelle shouldn't have been surprised—between the daily influx of tourists and Mei's stellar cooking, business boomed from morning until night. She paused at the entrance, jaw slack in mild shock.

"How can we even find a spot to talk in all this?" she quipped, sidling behind the counter to join Mei in the kitchen. She donned a disposable mask, gloves, and apron, grateful for her diner-honed ability to navigate a bustling food establishment. The heat from the multiple stovetops and the clatter of dishes reminded her of her old life—though on an even grander scale. Maybe *this* was the "new normal" in Sweetgum.

Mei, similarly masked and apron-clad, was kneading dough for dumplings. "No time to talk out there," she called over the hiss of the wok. "So we'll talk in here, *if* you can handle the hustle!" Despite the bustling chaos, there was a gleam of excitement in her eyes that told Rochelle how proud she was of her place.

Rochelle set to work, helping form dumplings. "I was going to ask how business is, but this tells me all I need to know." She shaped a dumpling and placed it on a tray, scanning the small army of waiters weaving in and out, and the cooks calling orders. "You look great, by the way. Mr. Zhang's locked away in his office, I bet?"

Mei's laughter was muffled by her mask. "He's handling paperwork. We've had so many new suppliers, new daily demands… I keep thinking, *Is this really Sweetgum?* Because it sure feels like a city these days."

Rochelle nodded, a pang of nostalgia tugging at her heart. "The tourism's not slowing, either. We're sharing Sweetgum with the whole world."

Mei shrugged. "And some folks want a *bigger* slice than we're willing to give." Her voice turned wry. "Any sign of those land developers who pestered you two?"

"Fewer of them," Rochelle admitted, "but it's still happening. Just last week, we said no to another big shot with a fancy briefcase. This week, though, it's been quiet. Maybe they're finally getting the hint." She rolled a piece of dough between her palms, shaping it carefully. "What about you? That one who showed up five days straight must've eventually gotten bored, huh?"

Mei's brow arched. "He never came back. Not once this week. It's like he vanished into thin air." Her tone was a mix of relief and suspicion. "But good riddance, I say. Nothing they offer is gonna pry this place from me."

Rochelle let out a relieved chuckle. "Same here. *Still,* it's odd they'd show so much interest and then just vanish."

"Think someone threatened them?" Mei joked with an exaggerated waggle of her eyebrows.

Rochelle's eyes widened in mock horror. "We're not that kind of town, Mei. The worst threat might be someone calling the cops for harassment."

Mei smirked, pressing the last dumpling into shape. "I guess that's more likely than an actual threat. Anyway—mystery solved or unsolved, I'm happy they're leaving us alone."

A comfortable silence fell as they focused on their cooking. The hiss of steam and the clang of ladles on metal echoed off tiled walls, and for a moment, Rochelle felt a wave of gratitude for the unchanging *essence* of Sweetgum. Yes, new businesses sprouted up like daisies in spring. Yes, more people strolled its streets every day. But beneath it all, the heart of this town—friendship, community, neighborly warmth—remained intact.

Mei broke the quiet with a hushed laugh. "At least life around here is never dull. Between your romance resort expanding and my restaurant thriving, who has time to get bored?"

Rochelle's lips curved, her mind darting to Benjamin's easy smile at breakfast. "Bored? We've never been more alive," she agreed softly. "Anyway," she added, glancing at the now-finished dumplings, "since we're done here, how about that walk you promised? I have gossip that'll make your head spin."

Mei's eyes gleamed. "Now, *that* is something I'm always ready for."

They pulled off their gloves and masks, returning to the front of the restaurant. Rochelle took a final look at the bustling room—*her friend's success, her own success, the unstoppable wave of life that had come to Sweetgum.* And she smiled.

Some things would never change, like her and Mei laughing over new rumors. But everything else? It was blossoming in ways Rochelle never could have foreseen—expanding, shifting, welcoming fresh possibilities. And she wouldn't have it any other way.

AUTHOR'S NOTE

Thank you so much for reading Reservations of the Heart, the tenth book in the Sweetgum Meadows Romance series of stand-alone novels. I really hope you loved it! If you enjoyed this book, please consider leaving a review so that others may also find it. Also, if you haven't read the first books yet, check them out today! Although these are stand-alone novels, the stories all intertwine and progress.

I look forward to introducing you to the other characters in this lovely, family-oriented town where each couple will find their happily ever after.

Would you like to receive bonus scenes and keep up with what's next with my upcoming books? Then, make sure you sign up for my mailing list on my website by visiting ImaniPrice.com.

My full audiobook catalog is available for FREE on YouTube. Check it out here: https://swiy.co/Sweetgum

ALSO BY IMANI PRICE

Book 1: Love Between Us

Book 2: Sweet Sunsets

Book 3: Infinite Kiss

Book 4: Dance With Me

Book 5: In Charge

Book 6: Forever With You

Book 7: Secret Sweethearts

Book 8: Endless Love

Book 9: The Harder We Fall

Book 10: Reservations of the Heart

Book 11: Play by Play

Book 12: Guarded Hearts

Book 13: Healing Hearts

Book 14: Dear Sweetgum

Book 15: Lanterns of the Meadows (novella)

Book 16: Drawn to You

Book 17: Under the Sweetgum Tree

Sweetgum Meadows' Visitor's Guide

To all my lovely readers,

Thank you for reading